Aislin

All-Hallows' Brides

Meara Platt

ARE YOU SIGNED UP FOR DRAGONBLADE'S BLOG?

You'll get the latest news and information on exclusive giveaways, exclusive excerpts, coming releases, sales, free books, cover reveals and more.

Check out our complete list of authors, too!

No spam, no junk. That's a promise!

Sign Up Here

www.dragonbladepublishing.com

Dearest Reader;

Thank you for your support of a small press. At Dragonblade Publishing, we strive to bring you the highest quality Historical Romance from the some of the best authors in the business. Without your support, there is no 'us', so we sincerely hope you adore these stories and find some new favorite authors along the way.

Happy Reading!

CEO, Dragonblade Publishing

Additional Dragonblade books by Author Meara Platt

The Book of Love Series
The Look of Love
The Touch of Love
The Taste of Love
The Song of Love
The Scent of Love
The Kiss of Love
The Hope of Love

Dark Gardens Series
Garden of Shadows
Garden of Light
Garden of Dragons
Garden of Destiny

The Farthingale Series
If You Wished For Me (A Novella)

Also from Meara Platt
Aislin

*** Please visit Dragonblade's website for a full list of books and authors. Sign up for Dragonblade's blog for sneak peeks, interviews, and more: ***
www.dragonbladepublishing.com

Dear Reader,

This story is inspired by Edgar Allan Poe's haunting poem, A Dream Within A Dream. My hero, William Croft, appeared as a character in an earlier story of mine called Pearls of Fire. He was found floating amid a ring of fire beside a sinking ship in the turbulent waters between England and Ireland. He was rescued but has no memory of the attack on his ship or the days leading up to it. Who was responsible? What happened to his brother? And who is Aislin, this girl who haunts his thoughts? This is William's story, a man whose life seems but a dream within a dream.

With love,
Meara

Chapter One

Cornwall, England
August, 1816

WILLIAM CROFT'S DREAMS lately had been of a girl with long dark hair always worn unbound and whose smoke-gray eyes had the power to reach into a man's soul. He saw her each night rushing down the steps of Tintagel Castle, a Celtic beauty from the myths of Merlin and Camelot and the dragon caves beneath the massive, stone ruins.

She now haunted his waking hours as well, to the point he could not move forward with his new life. Rather, it was a resumed life interrupted by years of memories lost.

"Will we reach Tintagel by sundown?" William Croft asked his coach driver when they stopped to rest the horses alongside an inland pool used as a watering hole for ponies that ran wild across Bodmin Moor.

"Aye, m'lord. Long before, never ye worry," the hired driver responded in a thick Cornish accent, deep and robust, almost swallowing the words as they rolled off his tongue.

A bleak expanse of heather stretched across the moor like waves upon a sea of palest lavender, their sturdy stalks tossed back and forth by the whipping wind. The vast emptiness was familiar to him, but he did not know why. He had no memory of ever crossing here before. Yet, he had been here, just as he had been to Tintagel Castle, Polzeath, and Port Isaac. His dreams lately had also been of these towns along the rugged Cornwall coast.

He shook his head to clear his thoughts, knowing he had surely lost his mind to come all this way from London for a girl who existed only in his fantasies. Was it possible she was real? She seemed so, and he knew he somehow had to find her in order to regain that lost part of himself.

The driver cleared his throat as he approached. "Baron Whitpool, the horses are ready."

He nodded to the burly Cornishman. "Let's make haste then, Mr. Musgrove."

Storm clouds were now gathering on the horizon, and he was eager to be on his way. This was an odd patch of land, seemingly devoid of life and yet herds of wild ponies roamed unfettered upon the moor. A falcon circled overhead, and in the distance, those purple-gray storm clouds swept ever closer, like winged dragons soaring upon the wind.

He climbed in the coach, feeling the sudden jolt as the matched bays lurched forward, and the wheels began to roll upon the rutted road.

Yes, he was eager to reach the castle before nightfall and find the girl.

He'd even given her a name in his dreams.

Aislin.

Did she exist?

Chapter Two

T HE SUN GLISTENED upon the ruined towers of Tintagel Castle as William hiked up the steps toward it later that afternoon. The turquoise ocean swirled beneath the pile of crumbled stone with powerful and deadly force. He heard the crash of waves against the cliff face and the roar as the wall of water swept into the hollow caves.

He'd spent the better part of an hour exploring these ruins in search of the girl. "Folly," he'd muttered to himself more than once. Still, he wanted to remain longer and search again around the tumbling castle and the cliff walks. But he was a practical man by nature and knew he ought first to settle his belongings at the inn his coachman's family ran in Boscastle.

He would return here tomorrow.

And the day after that.

As many days as necessary.

He also planned to ride to Polzeath and Port Isaac.

Not now, however. He was hot, and his throat was parched. One more turn through the remains of the castle and he'd be off, he decided with no small disappointment.

He walked back up the hill, breathing in the salty sea air that was so familiar and comforting to him.

He'd almost drowned in those turbulent waters, and yet he still loved it.

All his brothers had loved the sea, except Thomas, the eldest, who had first inherited the baronial title and the entailed estates that came along with it. Ironic that Thomas detested everything about the water, even though the family had gained its wealth from the shipping trade.

William was now Baron Whitpool since his brother's death. But before then, he had often sailed on his family's merchant fleet. Even after stepping into the title, he'd continued to sail, less frequently because of all the other Whitpool affairs that required his attention.

But the sea would never leave his soul.

Nor would Aislin, assuming she ever existed.

A bird cawed overhead.

He shaded his eyes and watched it spread its black wings against the azure sky. "A raven," he muttered, shaking his head as he continued to the castle, for they were often considered a bad omen.

He hurried along, even though the sun would remain high on the horizon well into the night. However, Boscastle would take an hour or more to reach.

He had to leave now to arrive in daylight.

Another few minutes and I'll go.

Were the other visitors presently wandering the grounds as fascinated as he was with this place? He expected they were, but for other reasons. They sought to tread where kings and mages of legend were rumored to have walked before them. Perhaps they imagined Merlin and Guinevere and the knights of King Arthur's court surrounding them and welcoming them into the castle.

He nodded to several ladies and gentlemen he encountered along the path. One of them was a frail looking man with a shock of white hair and a walking cane. But he'd managed to climb the steps, no feat possible unless one was relatively hale.

He watched the man hobble to a waiting carriage, then shrugged to dismiss him from his thoughts. He was more interested in finding the girl who'd led him here.

Even now, he felt the pull of his dreams as fiercely as an ocean tide.

Aislin, where are you?

His skin prickled.

The air around him began to sizzle.

How could he possibly sense her presence?

He shook out of the laughable thought.

And yet, he ached to find her and know she was real, for she was his only link to those lost memories.

As he approached one of the towers amid the ruins, a girl suddenly appeared in its archway. He blinked. She disappeared just as suddenly as she had come into sight. He would have thought nothing of it, only she had the look of Aislin, her hair long and dark and worn unbound. Those silken strands swirled around her body as the wind blew through them, just as he'd imagined in his dreams.

He ran toward the arch, but there was no sign of anyone by the time he reached it. He wanted to call out her name. *Aislin! Aislin!*

Everyone would believe he was mad to be chasing after a wraith.

Even he was no longer certain of his sanity.

In the next moment, he saw her again. This time, she was hurrying down the castle path overlooking the cliffs and ocean, her steps as light and graceful as a faerie flitting across a bluebell garden.

"Aislin!" he cried out, but his voice was swallowed amid the noise of the pounding waves that were thunderous and roaring as fiercely as his heart.

He ran after her.

AISLIN HURRIED DOWN the steps of Tintagel Castle toward the mare she'd left untethered to roam among the gorse and hedgerows overlooking the sand beach and rock cliffs. Why had she stayed so long? The sun was beginning to dip toward the horizon, and although it was still hours before nightfall, she had a long ride ahead.

She loved the sight of the ocean in its twilight glow, the way it cast a beautiful, silver sheen across the water. At this time of day, with the sun's rays hitting the water at just that angle, it seemed as though the ocean was covered in a sleek coat of ice.

However, it was merely an illusion. Beneath the shimmering surface roiled turbulent waves that could drag a man under and drown him in their powerful currents. A life lost, washed out to sea. All the while, the ocean would ebb and swell as ever before, the waves constant and ever breaking upon the shore.

She shook out of the morbid thought, knowing she had to hurry, or she would barely make it to Port Isaac before dark. Her father would be furious. He had business this evening, that's what he called it. *Business.* But it wasn't that at all. It was smuggling and piracy, and once murder because of her, he'd claimed.

He'd murdered to protect her, but she knew he'd done it to protect his own hide. It was easier to cast the blame on her.

Still, she fully felt the burden of blame, a soul-aching regret for a life cut short. The life of a good man. The very best sort, a man any young lady could love with all her heart given the chance. The irony of it was, she doubted her father's victim had ever given her a thought beyond asking for a pint of ale when she'd served his table at her father's establishment, the Farnsworth Inn.

Well, the gentleman had kissed her once, but out of gratitude and nothing more.

It all amounted to naught.

She hadn't been able to save him.

Aislin hurried across the bridge and down more steps, then broke into a run along the winding path when– "Sir! My apologies!" She'd slammed into a visitor to the castle ruins. He was big, and she'd careened straight into his broad chest.

Mother in heaven. This man was built like a warrior, his body as firm and unbending as Damascus steel.

She flailed her arms to regain her balance as she bounced off him, but he caught her by the waist and drew her close to steady her. She grabbed his arms and immediately felt the tension flowing through them.

"I do sincerely apologize." She must have hit him harder than she realized, knocking the wind out of him despite his size and obviously muscled strength. Ridiculously strong. His arms were boulders. "I..." The breath caught in her lungs.

William?

No, he was dead.

And yet, no matter how many times she blinked to correct her vision, he remained standing before her, the heat of his hands burning through the muslin of her gown. "It cannot be." He was just as she remembered him. Tall and broad-shouldered, his blond hair the color of beach sand, and dark green eyes that had once been light and smiling, but now appeared haunted and angry.

"You know me?" he asked, although it sounded more like a declaration, for there was a sharp edge to his voice that cut through her confusion like a finely-honed sword.

She could only nod in response.

Her heart was beating too fast, surging into her throat, and making speech impossible.

"Who am I?" He gave her a quick but gentle shake when she did not immediately reply. His hands were still about her waist, firm and unyielding. However, he touched her like a gentleman, taking care not to be rough as he held her.

Why would he not let go of her?

Did he believe she was a ghost who would disappear into the air if he dared release her? She feared to let go of him for the same reason.

Was he real?

How could he be? Her father had sworn he'd killed him.

Who am I? What an odd question to ask her. She tipped her head up to meet his steady gaze while she forced her breath to calm. She wasn't certain she'd found her voice yet, but she gave it a try. "You are Baron Whitpool. Are you not, my lord?"

Now, it was his turn to respond.

But he said nothing, only gazed at her unblinking.

"William Croft, fourth Baron Whitpool," she elaborated as the silence between them stretched uncomfortably. "Or is it fifth? I may have the count wrong. Perhaps it is third. Does it matter?"

"No, it doesn't matter," he said finally with a rasp to his voice.

His hands did not move from her waist.

The silence between them resumed.

She ought to have drawn away, or taken her hands off his arms, but she had no wish to let him go. Her heart still pounded too hard, and her legs were trembling so that she was no longer certain she could stand on her own.

William.

How could he be alive?

Yet, here he stood before her, as big and perfect as she remembered.

She would never address him as William among polite company…among any company, for that matter. She had no right to refer to him as anything but 'my lord' or 'Baron Whitpool'.

However, in the privacy of her thoughts she gave herself the liberty of calling him by his given name.

She studied him as boldly as he studied her.

Although he was a gentleman of rank, his appearance had never been genteel. There was an aura of power about him, a ruggedness in the build of his body and the strong line of his jaw. He was handsome back then, and even more so now.

His eyes were the green of emeralds.

"My lord, why have you come back?" She did not wish to sound alarmed, but he was in danger here. How could he not understand this?

"I had to," he said softly, the deep rumble of his voice almost a whisper.

"Why?"

He swallowed her up in his gaze. "To find you."

She laughed and shook her head in disbelief, recalling the day they'd first met. How long ago was it? Three years or more? It had taken her less than a minute to fall in love with him. That was the day he and his brother had marched into the Farnsworth Inn seeking rooms while they waited out a storm. What was the expression for the tingling, breathless feeling that had swept through her in that moment?

Love at first sight.

These same sensations came rushing back to her now, never truly lost, merely numbed because the ache in her heart was unbearable otherwise.

His brother Gideon had once bothered to ask her name. "Aislin," she'd replied, setting the mugs of ale they'd ordered on the table before them. William had never once looked up, never spoken to her, not even smiled at her.

Men were always smiling at her. She knew how to set them in their place.

Only later did he look at her.

And even then, it seemed such a small thing. Almost nothing.

But she'd felt his gaze as though a lightning bolt had shot through her body.

William's lips were now tightly pursed, and his brow remained furrowed as he continued to study her.

"You were looking for me?" she asked. "Do you even know *my* name?" The question may have come across as impertinent, but so was his continued silence and his frowning stare.

Aislin waited patiently for an answer, but still, he did not respond.

She could wait him out, for she was used to being on her own and speaking to no one. He was silent, but this place was alive with sound. Of waves crashing against the cliffs below. Of their roar and echo within the hollow caves.

Choughs and ravens cawed as they circled in the sky above, and the ever-present wind whistled through the ruins of Tintagel Castle.

"My name is Aislin," she said finally. "And why would you be looking for me?"

She felt a tremor shoot through him, for she still had her hands on him.

How odd they should continue to cling to each other, each afraid to let the other go. She understood her reasons, fear that she would lose him again.

His reasons?

Could they be anything other than revenge for what her father did to him?

"Aislin," he said in a husky murmur, circling an arm around her waist while he cupped her face in his warm hand with the other. *"My Aislin."*

He bent his head and kissed her softly on the mouth.

She wanted to cry for the beauty of it.

For the hunger of it.

His lips were warm and pleasantly firm. The kiss itself was not a polite kiss, but neither was it too rough. It seared her soul.

He'd kissed her like this once before.

She'd not forgotten and had never been in another man's arms since. In truth, she'd never been in a man's arms before his either. But it could not have meant anything to him back then. Did it mean anything now?

He was a baron. She was a barmaid.

Yet, he held her in his embrace as though she was his treasure.

She slid her hands up his broad chest to wrap her arms around his neck. As the kiss continued, she placed her hand against his cheek, feeling the rough bristle of a day's growth of beard. "How can I be *your* Aislin?" she asked when he drew his lips away.

"I don't know." He was not apologetic as he continued to hold her close, so that she felt his breath against her ear. "I hoped you might tell me."

"Me?" She stepped back and felt a chill when he released her. She grew angry that he might be playing a game with her. "Do you think you own me because I allowed you to kiss me once before?"

"I kissed you before this?" He shook his head as though reaching back for the memory.

So, he'd forgotten her. Then why go on about *my* Aislin now?

None of this made sense. Nor did her feelings for him, she supposed. "Yes, you kissed me. But only the one time before."

"When? I mean other than just now." He began to pace in front of her, then paused and ran a hand through his hair in obvious consternation. "When, Aislin?"

"Long ago. When you were last in Cornwall. As you were about to sail away."

"And that was...?"

"About three years ago. You came with your brother. He was polite, but you hardly said two words to me all the while you and he were here."

His body coiled with tension. She took another step back, for he appeared like a wolf about to pounce, savage and untamable. "You knew my brother?"

She nodded warily. "Gideon Croft. He hasn't come by here for over a month now. I thought perhaps you had come in his place."

He appeared quite shocked, his surprise a raw wound that had not yet healed. "Me? In his place?"

She put a hand to her throat. "Is he injured? Has he been harmed?"

He growled, the sound low and feral.

His gaze remained on her, fiery and so at odds for a man who'd just kissed her as gently as he had. She must have misunderstood. Of course, why would he feel any interest for her when he did not remember her?

He growled once more, the sound softer now but still angry. "What trick is this?"

He had her utterly confused. "How is my worrying about your brother any sort of trick?"

"My brother?" The words came out as an accusation as he repeated them slowly, his tone obviously wary. "Gideon?"

She nodded.

"You dare to claim you saw him recently?"

She stepped further back as he took another menacing step toward her. However, she did not fear that he would hurt her, even though his rage was as obvious as a gathering storm across the Irish Sea. "It's true. Let me think back, and I will tell you exactly when. But it was no more than two months ago, for certain."

"How is it possible? Our ship was attacked by pirates three years ago and sank in the St. George's Channel. I was the lone survivor. The *lone* survivor."

What irony, she thought bitterly.

Her father had meant to kill him alone.

Of course, this was her father's way, to destroy all who got in his path without a care for who they were or the harm caused to the innocents left behind to mourn their loss. Nor did he care that he might leave widows with small children to carry on by themselves. *I'm only after the goods*, he would tell her, and she forced herself to believe him. *We don't kill no one unless they come at us first. Only to defend ourselves, Aislin, m'love.*

"Why that look, Aislin? What do you find so hard to understand?" Something flared in his dark eyes. "No one else survived the pirate attack."

Her father had only mentioned killing him, even boasted about it. Never said a word about hurting others. She ought to have known he'd do away with anyone who could have pointed a finger at him. "I'm so sorry."

She meant it with all her heart.

In the darkest recesses of her mind, she had buried the truth. She'd suspected it, feared it, and then hidden the knowledge deep inside of her in order to pretend it had never happened. How could she be the blood of that monster?

He was her father, and she was ashamed of what he was.

She was ashamed of who *she* was, daughter to that man.

When he'd boasted of killing William, she knew in that moment Gentleman Jack Farnsworth had to be stopped. *Hah!* Gentleman was a misnomer, only given to him because he claimed to be the son of an earl. Born on the wrong side of the blanket, of course. "Then it is a mercy Gideon survived."

"Did you not hear what I just said? There were no survivors from my ship."

"I heard you, my lord. My heart is in pieces over it." She frowned as she studied his expression. Was it possible he did not remember? "You sent your brother off on other business before your vessel sailed. He never was aboard your ship. I saw him not two months ago."

A look washed over him, she could not tell whether he was surprised, relieved, or horrified. Likely every feeling tore through him in that moment. He grabbed her by the shoulders. "Tell me exactly where you saw him last."

"Right here, at Tintagel Castle. This is where I meet him." Her brow furrowed, now worried she'd given away too much information. But Gideon had always held his brother in the highest regard and…were they not on the same mission for the Crown? If not, then what had brought William here? "Why are you asking me these questions?"

He released her and once more ran a hand through his thick mane of hair. "Are you saying my brother is alive?"

"Yes, but you must know it. You're the one who sent him off to Plymouth for the militia. When you sailed out of Port Isaac, he was already on his way there to summon help."

He remained silent another long moment.

"My lord, I will meet you here tomorrow if you wish. But I must leave now. Where are you staying?"

"Nowhere settled yet."

She thought he might be lying to her, for gentlemen always sent on ahead for rooms to be made ready wherever they traveled. Perhaps he'd come here in haste and hadn't made arrangements. "Do not go near Port Isaac or Polzeath. They'll kill you if they see you there. Head north, my lord. You'll be safer in Trevalgo or Boscastle. You mustn't come south."

"Who'll kill me?"

She couldn't tell him. Not until she knew more about William's purpose. Likely, it was to kill her father. Jack Farnsworth deserved it, too, for all the evil he had done. But Gideon's orders from the Crown were to gather enough evidence to disrupt and destroy the operations of the pirates who plundered in the waters off Cornwall.

Gentleman Jack wasn't the only devil to loot and pillage along the coast, only among the most ruthless. Also, there was a high-ranking traitor in their midst who had to be ferreted out.

She would not be the one to ruin years of Gideon's work.

"Aislin, who are you to my brother?"

"Me?" She shook her head and laughed softly. "I'm no one to him, not in the way I think you are implying."

Was it relief she noticed in his eyes?

She glanced away to look at the sky and knew she ought to be on her way. The days were long in summer, but she had a lengthy ride home and would be making the last leg in the dark if she did not leave soon.

But leaving William was no easy thing to do.

She'd just found him again and could not bear to lose him. "My lord, why did you kiss me?"

"In truth, I don't know. Perhaps I was listening to my heart."

"Your heart?"

He nodded, seeming to be in earnest.

What a lark!

"Baron Whitpool, who do you think I am to you?"

Chapter Three

W ILLIAM DID NOT know how to answer the question Aislin had posed.

Who do you think I am to you?

Someone important, she had to be. If only he could remember. But his memories of that time were lost, still trapped in a thick mist that hovered over a vital part of his brain. Finding Aislin had done nothing to clear it away.

Too soon, perhaps.

He had to be patient. Give it time.

But there had been so much time lost already.

For the last three years, William had been known as Lucifer by the sailors who'd found him floating amid a ring of fire from the debris of a sinking ship in St. George's Channel just south of the Irish Sea.

It was a favorite stalking ground for the Cornish pirates.

Aislin was somehow connected to those pirates and the attack on his ship, but he did not know how. For all he knew, she could have been the one to order his vessel destroyed. But his dreams of her had never been angry or distrustful ones.

Quite the opposite, his every instinct had been to protect her.

Even now, he sensed the girl was in danger. Obviously, more so because of his presence here. "Aislin, in truth, I do not know what we are to each other. But I cannot shake the feeling you are important to me. I have no memory of my time here. I need your help. You must tell me truthfully. Who are you?"

And why have I been dreaming of you?

Her lips were full and delicately shaped, but pinched in a thin, straight line as she shook her head. "No. You'll get no more from me today. I'll meet you here tomorrow."

"Tomorrow? Why not now?" He searched her face as though wondering whether she could be trusted or not.

"Because I must go."

"Where? How will I find you if I need to get word to you?"

She frowned. "You won't. I'll seek you out. Promise you will not follow me."

"Only if you promise you'll return here tomorrow."

"I will, my lord. I'll try my best." She looked around, wondering whether her own father had ordered her followed. "If not tomorrow, then the day after. I am not always free to come and go as I wish."

She glanced around again.

"Aislin, are you afraid you are being watched?"

"No, not anymore. I was at first, but that was years ago. They all trust me now."

"Who is *they*?"

She ignored the question, knowing it was up to Gideon to tell him. Where was Gideon? And how could his own brother not know he was alive?

"Will you be harmed if we're found together?" he asked, catching her by surprise for the sincerity of his concern. "Who will harm you?"

She purposely frowned at him, hoping to dissuade him from doing anything foolish. "Just do not come south. You may not have a care for your own life, but if you value mine at all, then do as I say. Even the towns north of here may not be safe for you. Keep to yourself. Try not to draw any notice. You'll have to trust me."

She'd been riding here for at least a year before William's brother had ever attempted to contact her. And three years since William was believed drowned. Her father had long ago stopped worrying about her comings and goings. He was not about to waste a man to follow her around when he believed she was half mad and running off to be alone with her wild thoughts.

Nor did he trust his men to keep their hands off her.

She knew she was pleasing to a man's eye. Many had called her beautiful, but she did not feel beautiful inside.

She felt ashamed for all those years of doing nothing while her father destroyed lives.

He'd been quite secretive about it, at first.

Now, he was bold as brass about his 'privateering' as he called it.

If any good had come out of her acceptance of his business, it was that her father now trusted her. After three years…three long years of playing the role of docile daughter, he was convinced she would never betray him.

A shiver ran through her.

Perhaps he knew her better than she knew herself.

Yes, she was determined to help put an end to the piracy rampant in the area. It was one thing to smuggle goods and to allow those ships and their crewmen to sail away in peace. But to mercilessly sink a ship and watch all those helpless souls aboard drown?

The thought was too horrible to contemplate.

Yet, did she have the strength of will to betray her father? To point a finger at him? Testify against him? Allow him to be hanged?

He deserved far worse.

Still, he was the one who'd sired her and raised her. Could she be the one to send him to the gallows?

"Very well, Aislin. I'll trust you."

She nodded, silently hoping his faith in her was not misplaced.

She returned to her mare, about to climb onto the saddle when she felt William's hands at her waist once more, this time to help her up.

He released her as soon as she was settled, and then gave her mare a friendly stroke along her neck. "Safe travels, Aislin."

"Thank you."

He cast her a wry smile. "I don't think you needed my help getting into the saddle, but…"

"I know." He needed this last touch to be certain she was real. "I'll wake tomorrow wondering whether I dreamed you up, too."

THE PENDRAGON INN at Boscastle was a pleasant surprise, much nicer than William had expected. Mr. Musgrove, his jovial driver, had gone on and on about the place, assuring him it was one of the finer establishments in the area. He'd dismissed the man's rambling, but he had to admit, Mr. Musgrove had not been exaggerating.

The inn more resembled a country manor. It was sturdily built of local stone, had attractively painted blue shutters, several chimney stacks, and red roses lining its garden path to a front door that was also painted blue.

Beyond it and off to the side was a well maintained stable and carriage house.

Indeed, the place appeared quite charming.

Mr. Musgrove's sister and her husband welcomed him inside, giving him a bit of history as he entered. "They've run the inn for the past twenty years, m'lord," Mr. Musgrove said.

William nodded politely as he was introduced to John Sloane and his wife, Anne, an older woman who bore a striking family resemblance to his driver, down to the same amiable smile and barrel-shaped body.

"M'father ran the inn before me," John Sloane said with an obvious ring of pride, "and m'grandfather before that."

The aroma of roasted game hen and bread fresh out of the oven penetrated William's senses as he was shown to the common room. "We serve our guests their meals here," Mrs. Sloane said. "M'lord, would ye care to relax by the hearth with a tankard of ale while my brother brings yer bags up to yer chamber?"

He accepted the offer. "However, I would rather dine alone this evening."

The woman bobbed her head. "I'll have yer supper brought up to yer chamber as soon as it's ready. Ye're to have our finest, m'lord."

The ale was just what he needed to slake his thirst. He'd just drained his tankard when Mrs. Sloane returned to lead him upstairs. He followed her as she lumbered up the creaking steps.

Mr. Musgrove followed with the last of his bags.

William usually traveled light. However, not this time. He wasn't certain how long he'd be required to remain in the area, so he'd brought perhaps too much. He had come here determined not to leave until he'd found Aislin.

That he'd come upon her already had caught him by surprise. He hadn't expected the search to be so easy, certainly not to meet with success on his first visit to Tintagel Castle.

That she was real had also surprised him.

He was more than a little relieved to know he was not going mad. Yet, there were still so many questions left to be answered.

Aislin was clearly the cornerstone.

But how? Why? And did he dare trust her?

He sank onto the bed in order to remove his boots, but Mr. Musgrove took it upon himself to assist him. He knelt in front of William. "Let me do that fer ye, m'lord."

William made no protest, for his mind was still awhirl. Aislin was real, and he'd found her, he thought for the hundredth time since they'd run into each other.

However, finding her had not restored his memory. Quite the opposite, it left him more befogged than ever, raising more questions, and not providing the answers he sought.

However, the girl had proved to be soft flesh and warm blood. The tug to his heart was even stronger now.

Painful, in truth.

This is what the romantic poets wrote about, the ache that tore at a man's soul.

He shook out of the thought to consider what Aislin had told him about Gideon. Could he trust what she'd said about his being alive?

How could it be true?

And yet, he wanted so desperately to believe her.

As Mr. Musgrove continued to fuss about the room, William rose to stare out the window onto the street below. At this twilight hour, there were few people on the streets. Boscastle was a quiet town with none of the bustle of London. There was no smart set here, no *haute ton* who amused themselves with idle entertainments well into the night.

Aislin had mentioned she would often meet Gideon at Tintagel Castle. Since she'd also warned it was dangerous for him to go to Port Isaac or Polzeath, he expected she'd issued the same warning to Gideon.

If so, was it possible Gideon hid out here? Or used Boscastle as an occasional safe harbor for his operations, or whatever he was supposedly doing on behalf of the Crown? If so, he would be known in Boscastle.

More important, someone here might know how to get word to him.

He'd question the Sloanes and their staff.

However, he did not expect they would offer promising leads. He and Gideon were brothers and resembled each other. But there had been no sign of recognition, no curious looks that he could discern beyond *what is a baron doing here?*

It also stood to reason that if Gideon was using Boscastle for his operations, he would not be staying in the fanciest inn or involving himself with reputable people.

Which meant William had to get himself to the disreputable part of town.

He'd do it this evening, slip out to investigate once all had quieted. If there was something sinister going on, it would happen under cover of darkness.

His door had been left slightly ajar. He was just about to stride across the room to close it when he heard a clomping on the stairs. Mr. Musgrove did not appear to pay any notice to the person whose footsteps had suddenly stilled in the hallway immediately outside his door. William reached for his pistol and crossed his chamber to swing it open, his weapon at the ready but held out of sight.

"Good day, Baron Whitpool." Standing before him was the white-haired gentleman he'd seen earlier at Tintagel Castle.

"Good day to you, sir." William tightened his grasp on the weapon discretely hidden behind his back.

He didn't like coincidences.

"This is your room?" the man asked, suddenly looking about as if addled.

"It is. Forgive me, sir. But you have me at a disadvantage. You know my name."

"Ah, but you are all the young maids are talking about." He shook his head and gave a wheezing chuckle. "Mr. Worthington, at your service. Reginald Worthington. You're new to the area, I hear. Seems to me, you know your way around quite well. I saw you with that dark-haired girl earlier today. Aislin is her name."

22

William ignored the comment.

Worthington's smile disappeared and he leaned closer. "Watch out for her, my lord. She's dangerous, that one is. You'd best keep away from her."

"Why?"

"Well, it isn't for me to gossip. Have a good evening, Baron Whitpool." The man turned and walked with shuffling footsteps to his door.

William watched the fellow, waited to hear the click of his latch, and for him to enter the room directly across the hall.

He rubbed his neck, for the short hairs were standing on end.

He didn't like this Worthington fellow. Who was he? And why the pretense of frail health? He'd heard him on the stairs. Solid footsteps. No weak shuffle. He'd also climbed the steps at Tintagel Castle, no easy feat for anyone in ill health.

He'd have to watch him, William decided, tucking his pistol away.

Mr. Musgrove quirked an eyebrow upon noticing William's continued frown. "M'lord, is something amiss?"

"No." He paused a moment. "What do you know of the girl I met at the castle ruins?"

"A pretty lass, ain't she?" His chortle resonated deep within his chest. "She's Jack Farnsworth's daughter. I'd stay away from her if ye know what's healthy for ye."

"Why?"

"It ain't m'place to say, m'lord."

"Say it anyway." He needed to learn all he could about Aislin, for she was important to him.

"I've heard trouble follows her. I wouldn't get too close if I were ye."

He asked a few more questions, then changed the topic in the hope of learning more about his brother. But he quickly realized Mr. Musgrove had said all he intended to say. No matter. He'd ask the innkeeper and his wife. He'd also ask the staff a few discreet questions, mostly about Gideon.

He expected that quizzing them about Aislin would yield the same responses he'd just received. Two warnings. Worthington and Musgrove. Still, he had to ask. Their comments had left him troubled. Did any of the maids know her? What did the staff think of her?

Yes, they would know her.

She was exceptionally pretty.

Men did not ever forget a face such as hers.

He certainly hadn't, despite forgetting everything else.

There was something special about this girl.

She had a way of looking at him, as though able to see straight into his soul. She did not appear evil. Quite the opposite, she seemed warm and genuine. He wanted to believe she was. After all, what reason would she have to lie to him about herself or Gideon?

And yet, more to the point and a reminder for caution, what reason would she have to tell him the truth?

Chapter Four

"**M**'LORD, DO YE need anything more?" Mr. Musgrove asked, interrupting his thoughts.

"No, thank you. Enjoy your time with your sister. I won't have need of you for the rest of the evening."

William waited for the man to leave his chamber before stretching out on the bed and closing his eyes. He meant to do more thinking, but a feeling he could only describe as relief suddenly washed over him like a crushing wave.

He sat up and buried his face in his trembling hands. What was happening to him? Tears began to fall. *My little brother is alive.*

For three years, he'd believed Gideon dead. But he was alive. Aislin had told him so. He dared not trust the news, but the hope of it overwhelmed him. He could not hold back his tears of joy. That he had any tears left to spill surprised him.

After all these years and all he'd been through.

Until this very moment, he did not think he had the capacity ever to hope or feel again.

Gideon. He wanted to see him and hug him fiercely.

Then he wanted to pummel the thoughtless idiot to the ground for leaving their sister to fend for herself. All those years struggling on her own, poor Abby. She thought she'd lost three brothers. Thomas, Gideon, and himself. As if it weren't bad enough, their youngest brother had returned home from war a battered and broken man.

Why hadn't Gideon come forward then?

Abby had been in desperate straits and needed help to deal with Peter.

Why didn't you claim the title, Gideon?

Gideon would have been next in line after him to become Baron Whitpool. If he was truly alive, then why hadn't he come forward to claim his birthright? Even if he hadn't wanted the elevated status—which still made no sense—he should have sent word to the family. Something. A consoling letter to Abby upon learning of his drowning.

Why hadn't Gideon reached out to her back then?

And what of their youngest brother? It had been cruel to allow Peter to believe he was the last surviving brother and had come into the title. Of course, he now knew the truth. But back then, the responsibility had weighed on him like Atlas shouldering the world. Gideon ought to have known how difficult it would be for Peter, who was too sick in body and soul to manage anything.

"Blast it," he said in a strained whisper. "Gideon, where are you?"

There had to be good reason for his abandoning the family.

But William could not think of a single excuse.

Fortunately, Abby had landed on her feet. She'd met her husband, Tynan Brayden, Earl of Westcliff, when he'd come to her rescue and helped her out with Peter. They might never have met, if not for her struggles.

But it still did not absolve Gideon from the pummeling he deserved.

William had just used his sleeve to wipe away the last of his tears when he heard a gentle knock at the door. His hand immediately went to the pistol he kept tucked in his jacket.

"Enter," he called and stood to watch as the innkeeper and his staff traipsed in. Mr. Sloane and one of his assistants hauled the tub into his chamber. Two maids came in behind him, toting pails of hot water. He smiled. He hated bathing in cold water.

One of the maids misunderstood his smile and cast him a hungry look.

Mrs. Sloane came in soon after, carrying his supper tray. Game hen and leeks. And a bottle of wine with which to wash them down. "Maisie, don't dawdle."

Ah, that was the girl's name.

He'd question Maisie later, for she had an *accommodating* look about her.

He sank into his chair and casually poured himself a glass of wine, smuggled in from France no doubt.

It was these niceties that kept the local pirates safe from arrest. Indeed, William knew he'd have to be careful when dealing with the local magistrates and military commanders. Most of them were likely among the first corrupted by promises of French lace and fine wines, Irish glassware, Italian silks and velvets, and other luxuries looted from merchant vessels sailing along the coast.

"Let me know if you need anything more, m'lord," Maisie said, leaning over as she poured her pail of water into his tub to give him a clear view down her bodice. Her meaning was unmistakable, for the girl did not seem to understand subtlety.

She ambled past him, bending over to wipe at an imaginary spot of dust on the table beside his glass of wine.

Her breasts rubbed against his shoulder.

When he was once more left alone, he quickly washed and ate, then donned fresh clothes. It was late now, well past ten o'clock and the soft, golden light had given way to a starry night. He plumped his pillows and laid them out under his bedcovers to make it appear he was sleeping should anyone look in.

He went downstairs to the inn's taproom, intending to ask questions there first. Next, he would move on to one of the local taverns.

But the Sloanes had closed up early. All was quiet. The other guests must have retired to their own quarters, for no one was moving about. Not a single floorboard creaked, other than those under his boots.

The inn was frequented mostly by well-heeled guests coming from outside Cornwall. Few were Londoners who were used to keeping late hours. Then he heard a creaking overhead. Mr. Worthington's room...into the hall...pause...back into his room. Where was this gentleman from? He hadn't mentioned it in conversation.

It mattered little, he supposed.

He'd come here to find Aislin, and he would now remain a while longer to investigate Gideon's disappearance. A brother resurrected and immediately lost again.

If Worthington continued to act suspiciously, he'd ask the innkeepers more about him.

The renewed silence unsettled him.

Suddenly, he heard the creak of a door in the direction of the servant's quarters. He turned just as Maisie popped her head in the taproom, candle in hand.

She giggled. "Were ye lookin' for me, m'lord?"

She came toward him, wearing only a thin nightrail that hid very little of her full figure. The linen was sheer, revealing the dusky coloring around her nipples and the dark patch at the junction of her legs. One sleeve had slipped off her shoulder so that the fabric was held up only by the lushness of her breasts.

"Sit with me a moment, will you Maisie?"

"On yer lap?" She seemed eager to oblige.

"No, I only wish to talk to you." Perhaps he was being an idiot for not taking the girl up on her sexual advances. He wanted answers, and she was the sort of girl who seemed willing to supply them if he obliged by pleasuring her in return.

"What shall we talk about?" She rubbed her breasts against his arm again and purred like a cat licking cream out of a bowl.

To touch this girl felt like a betrayal of Aislin.

Blessed saints. When had he turned into a monk?

She took his hand and guided it between her legs.

"I only wish to talk," he repeated, easing out of her grasp.

She frowned. "Do ye not like women, m'lord? My cousin Collin will gladly service ye."

"I don't require *servicing*, Maisie."

She tossed him a practiced pout. "It's that Aislin, isn't it? We heard ye'd met her at the castle."

"What do you know of her?" Yes, to touch this girl when he only wished to touch Aislin, was betrayal. Aislin was real and had meant something to him three years ago...just what, he did not know.

Something special, for he'd remembered her while all else was forgotten.

She meant something to him still. Despite the warnings received from Musgrove and Worthington, she was in his heart, and he could not keep away from her.

But he wanted to know more about her. Needed to know more. Where to start? He had so many questions to ask this silly girl.

Musgrove said Aislin was dangerous, and he ought to keep away.

As for Worthington, he did not trust anything the man said.

He repeated the question. "Tell me, Maisie. What do you know of Aislin?"

Her eyes rounded in fear. "I don't know nothing about 'er. Men die around 'er is all I know, so ye'd be best keepin' yer distance from that one."

She turned and fled back into the servant quarters.

Damn it.

Was he the only fool who trusted Aislin? Well, he wanted to

trust her…it wasn't quite the same thing.

Shrugging, he decided to venture into Boscastle. Perhaps he'd pick up some local gossip that would prove more useful, especially about Gideon. Since there was no further conversation to be had here, he slipped quietly through the inn's kitchen door and made his way into the village.

He wasn't certain where to head first, but his instincts had led him to Aislin, so he was going to trust those same instincts to lead him somewhere interesting now. He dismissed his botched encounter with Maisie for the moment.

And Musgrove's warning.

And Worthington's lies.

The moon stood out against the star-filled sky like a giant silver ball as he made his way silently through the streets. Moonlight cast enough of a glow to illuminate the town square and the quaint row of houses surrounding it.

A few homes had fires lit. He could smell the smoke wafting from their chimneys toward him on the cool breeze.

He hurried down a main road that cut through the heart of town. The respectable shops were shut at this hour. He noticed a lone torchlight emanating from a tavern at the very end of the street.

He debated whether or not to enter, but his instincts were on alert again, warning him not to go in. However, he had no intention of returning to the inn. He decided to stand in the shadows and observe who walked in and out of the tavern.

He would enter later, if someone or something caught his interest.

Despite his boredom, he kept his attention trained on the tavern door. He overheard several conversations as men were leaving and entering. Mostly, it was local farmers discussing this year's crops.

He took notice of two finely dressed gentlemen walking in.

He edged closer, for this was not the sort of place frequented by the better classes. Why were these men here? For purposes of smuggling? After all, even smugglers were businessmen of a sort and would have to make plans with their shady contacts somewhere. This tavern was as good a place as any.

Who were they? A wealthy landowner? A magistrate? One of the local military commanders out of uniform to hide his nefarious purpose?

Perhaps one of them was Gideon.

No. Even though the torchlight distorted their faces, casting them half in shadow and half in glaring firelight, he'd still know his brother anywhere. Neither man had Gideon's features. Their bodies were not shaped like Gideon's either.

These were smaller men.

He and Gideon were big and broad shouldered.

The night wore on, and the tavern owner finally closed up. William returned to his room at the Pendragon Inn, irritated that he had nothing to show for this night's prowling.

Well, it had only been one night.

Luck had been on his side when finding Aislin.

But neither smugglers nor pirates, nor even one's brother, appeared with the snap of one's fingers merely because one wished them to. Unfortunately, it would likely be weeks before anyone did anything suspicious.

Or helpful to his investigation.

He opened his chamber door and instantly felt a shiver run up his spine.

Something was amiss.

After giving the room a quick inspection, he stepped in. His eyes had become accustomed to the darkness hours ago, allowing him to prowl like a cat about town. So, he had no trouble making out the shapes and shadows now. His tension eased after a search revealed no intruder was hiding in wait for him.

The room appeared to be untouched, the tray of food exactly where he'd left it on the small table by the window. The half empty bottle of wine still stood beside his goblet. He lit a candle and set it on the small night table beside the bed. He was about to sink onto the mattress when he noticed why he continued to feel unease.

The covers and the pillows he'd stuffed beneath them to mimic the shape of a man were torn.

Not merely torn, he realized, feeling along the linen.

They were slashed with a knife.

Slashed as if someone had stabbed the pillows repeatedly.

"Bloody hell," he muttered.

Someone had come into his chamber intending to kill him.

But who?

Blessed saints.

Was it Aislin?

Chapter Five

W ILLIAM SLEPT FITFULLY through the night.
He'd placed his table against the door and set his wash
basin and ewer so that they were precariously balanced on the edge
of it. All would come toppling down with a clatter if anyone
attempted to nudge open his door.

He'd also placed the wine bottle, goblet, and tray of food immediately under the window so that anyone climbing in would step
on them, causing them to fall and shatter.

With all access duly secured, no one could surprise him.

Still, he slept lightly and woke constantly. That someone had
attempted to kill him was obviously troublesome.

What bothered him most was that it might have been Aislin.

Who else knew he was here?

Well, in truth, it could have been anyone. Even one of the
seemingly harmless visitors to Tintagel Castle yesterday.

Worthington.

Prime suspect.

But what was his motive?

Anyone in Boscastle could have done it, for that matter. Gossip
traveled fast, and this was a small town. Everyone would know of
his arrival by now, for he was a baron, and that in itself was news.

Maisie would tattle for certain.

The girl could not keep her legs or her mouth shut.

Bah! He was out of sorts and passing judgement on the poor maid. What right did he have? He was an oddity in this place. And he certainly was no saint. Nor had he slipped into town quietly. No, indeed. He'd arrived in a carriage and brought along bags enough to last him through an entire season.

Anyone could have spread the word. The ostler, the black-smith, or one of the inn's servants. Maisie came to mind again, not in any good way.

He chided himself for even bothering to question her.

In truth, she puzzled him. This was a respectable establishment, and yet she hadn't hesitated to offer her 'services' to him. Perhaps it was harmless, but what if she'd offered herself up as a means to pry information out of him?

If so, who had paid her to do it?

What had he said to the girl? *Nothing.* He'd been too busy rebuffing her advances.

He'd mentioned Aislin.

"Aislin," he muttered, recalling how the mere mention of her name frightened everyone. He half expected Maisie to make the sign of the cross and toss holy water at him when next they met.

Perfect. The last thing he needed was an entire community believing he was possessed by a witch.

His thoughts returned to the attempt to take his life...or on his pillows if one wanted to be precise about it. Who meant to do him harm? Someone who did not wish him to leave Cornwall alive.

William rose at cock's crow to wash and shave but waited until the servants had begun to stir before dressing and heading downstairs.

"Good mornin', m'lord," Mrs. Sloane said, greeting him with a merry smile. "Going to be another fine day, it appears."

He nodded. "It does seem so."

He watched as she bustled about the common room, readying

the tables for the breakfast offered to their guests. All meals were provided by the innkeepers, for there was nowhere else in town to dine other than the local tavern he'd been scouting last night. It drew a less fashionable crowd, and no lady would ever step foot in there.

"Mrs. Sloane, who has access to the rooms upstairs?"

She set down the stack of plates in her arms and turned to him. "Why, just my staff and the guests who let rooms here." She frowned thoughtfully. "Is there a problem, m'lord? Is something of yours missing?"

"No, nothing's been taken. However, someone entered my room last night."

Her expression noticeably eased. "Well, it could have been one of the maids to turn down your bed."

"No, Mrs. Sloane. Nothing as innocent as that. Someone entered who meant to kill me." He ought to have spoken to her husband about it, or mentioned it to Mr. Musgrove first, but she'd struck him as an honest woman, and he was curious to see her expression when he told her.

He felt badly about it now, for she'd turned pale and her expression was one of utter and complete shock. It was not well done of him, but he'd learned something from her response. Neither she nor her husband had a hand in this. "Will you summon Mr. Sloane and Mr. Musgrove for me?"

She nodded and scurried out.

It did not take long before both men stood before him in the common room. Mr. Sloane was wringing his hands and his pallor was ashen. "My lord, nothing like this has ever happened here before. Whatever you want. Whatever you need. We are at your service."

"Your staff, Mr. Sloane. How well do you know them?"

"Why, all of them since birth. The maids are nieces of mine."

Oh, lord. Maisie is his niece?

"Our cook is my sister. As for our taproom, either I do the serving or my brother does. His boys, Collin and Ethan, help out with the bags and any repairs or heavy chores that need to be done. We are a family establishment of the highest repute."

He nodded. "The inn's guests then?"

Mr. Sloane did not hesitate to show him the register.

No one stood out as suspicious, not even Mr. Worthington who was registered in the room across from his, and whose heavy footfalls had caught his notice last night. He appeared to be a regular visitor to the inn, his name appearing often in the register. Still, he had to ask. "Oh, m'lord, Mr. Worthington's been coming here for years to take the cure. But he took ill last night, and Maisie had to sit up with him for much of the night. She doesn't mind. He pays her extra for it."

William smothered his groan. He didn't think Maisie sat up with the man as much as lay flat on her back for him.

"You say he takes the cure? I would think Bath would be the place for him."

Mr. Sloane shook his head. "We are not quite as well known, but it is said the waters around Tintagel Castle are good for one's bones. Poor Mr. Worthington. He isn't a well man. He comes regularly to drink the waters and seek treatment from Dr. Jones."

"Jones?"

"Yes, m'lord. He's the best doctor for miles around. You'll find him in Trevena, only a stone's throw from the castle."

Mr. Musgrove stood beside him, scratching his thick head of gray hair. "I can't imagine who would do this. I'll ask around, m'lord. The locals may not open up to you, but they'll speak freely to me. We'll get to the bottom of this nasty business."

Mr. Sloane nodded. "We keep the doors securely latched at night. Anyone coming in after hours has to ring the bell. If this villain had run off after doing the wicked deed, something would have been left open or unlatched. A door. A window."

William had crept out the kitchen door and come back in that way. He'd made certain to secure that access once he'd returned. But someone could have seen him leave and used that unlatched kitchen door. There would be no trace because William had latched it again himself upon returning.

If his assailant had seen him leave, then why bother to enter his bedchamber and stab an empty bed?

More questions raised and none answered.

Still, it could not hurt to ask about other possible routes of access. "Is there a secret panel or door leading out?" This area was rife with smuggling. He expected almost every structure in this town had hidden tunnels or passageways used to haul goods in and out without being seen.

That moment's hesitation told William all he needed to know.

To most people in these parts, smuggling was a necessity, not a crime. The taxes imposed on their everyday goods and small luxuries were too high. Since the war with France had been going on for years with all French products banned until quite recently, they'd had to make their way to England somehow. Women wanted their perfumes and lace. Men wanted their fine wines.

Someone had to provide it.

Why not the good citizens of Cornwall?

He sighed and shook his head. "Yes, Mr. Musgrove, do ask around town. See if you can turn up anything about last night's business."

"Aye, m'lord."

As for him, he was returning to Tintagel Castle. Since Mr. Sloane kept several handsome horses in his stable, William chose to borrow a sturdy stallion by the name of Destiny. He was a beast with an ebony coat and obsidian eyes that were so dark and evil-looking, Devil might have been a more appropriate name for him.

It was still morning by the time he rode from Boscastle to the Tintagel Castle ruins. Mr. Musgrove went off as well, but to gather whatever information he could from the locals who trusted him as they would never trust William.

He urged Destiny to a gallop, for he was eager to see Aislin again, even if she proved to be the assailant who intended to kill him.

What would he do then?

He couldn't simply shrug off her possible involvement, not even if his instincts told him the girl did not have a violent bone in her body.

However, she kept secrets.

That alone ought to have made him wary of her. What did he know of Aislin? She'd only appeared to him in his dreams.

His heartbeat quickened as he rode past the hamlet of Trevena, and Tintagel Castle came into view. Although the castle was nothing more than piles of rock and rubble surrounded by sheep grazing in the nearby meadows, there was still something exquisitely majestic about its archways and crumbling towers and the turquoise sea that flowed beneath it.

He tethered Destiny at the spot where Aislin had left her mare yesterday, and then strode to the cliff edge to gaze out upon the water while waiting for the girl. The sight of Tintagel's dark stone walls thrust out on an outcropping, as though daring the tide waters to swallow it up, quite moved him.

The castle was a ruin, yet life abounded around this place.

Shepherds drove their sheep to the flower-dotted meadows. Coachmen drove curious travelers to the castle and then back to whichever inn they were staying for the night. A local pieman had set up a stall nearby to sell his pasties and Cornwall's special cream tea for those who were thirsty.

The quaint village of Trevena could be seen in the distance.

Life in these parts was simple, to be sure.

All who lived around here, shepherds and coachmen, blacksmiths and tailors, thatchers and bakers and millers, seemed not to care that kings and knights of legend were reputed to have crossed these meadows and marched up these timeless steps.

"Lord Whitpool," came a soft voice from behind him.

He turned to find Aislin smiling at him.

Despite his misgivings about the girl, he could not help but return her smile. "Good morning, Aislin."

"A lovely day, isn't it, my lord?" She did not hide her delight in seeing him. In truth, her expression was a ray of sunlight that filled the darkest recesses of his heart.

Was he blinded by his attraction to her?

Had Gideon felt the same, and she'd killed him?

"No," he muttered, wanting to trust her despite all the reasons he should not. How could she have been the one to steal into his room at the inn and plunge the dagger into his pillows? Would he not have caught the scent of lavender—her scent—in the air?

She laughed merrily in confusion. "Did you just say it was *not* a lovely day, my lord?"

She glanced up at the blue sky and white puffs of clouds that dotted it. The sun shone down in all its splendor, causing the waters below them to sparkle like glitter. The breeze was warm and gentle.

He grinned sheepishly. "It is lovely. I was just remembering something I had forgotten to do. I'm sure my coach driver will take care of it. Nothing important." It was a vague enough lie.

She nodded and looked out toward the sea, seeming not at all surprised to find him alive. Nor did she appear to be angry or worried that he might become suspicious of her after the failed attempt.

What he saw in the soft gray of this girl's eyes was...well, it was something he could not easily describe. She was happy to see him, but it was more than that. If he were a coxcomb, he'd say the girl was more than a little infatuated with him.

Hell.

Had he lain with her all those years ago?

Had he made promises to her that he had no intention to fulfill?

It wasn't in his nature to lure a woman into his bed with lies and false promises. Perhaps his nature had been different back then.

He didn't like to think so.

Would this fog on his memory never lift?

"Shall we walk to the ruins?" he asked, his frustration mounting along with the desire to take this girl into his arms and kiss her endlessly.

What had Aislin meant to him in the past? Something pure and beautiful, it had to be. She looked at him with such joy, such innocence.

He had not bedded Aislin.

He was certain of it.

But he sorely ached to do so now. More to his shame or his stupidity, if she had been the one to stab his pillows.

"Yes, my lord. Let's walk over there. We'll be safer behind the castle walls. Anyone can see us standing out here in the open."

"May I take your arm as we walk?" He did not know why he could not rid himself of this compelling need to touch her.

He knew she was real and no illusion.

She appeared surprised, but pleased. "Yes, of course you may."

He held out his arm, enjoying the light touch of her hand as she rested it on his forearm.

"I cannot stay long today, my lord." She nibbled her lower lip. "My father wants me home early."

He forced his gaze from her lips. "Why? Is something going on that I should know about?"

She paused at the bottom of the steps. "It is something your brother should be told about. But I don't know where he is or how to get word to him." She cast him an imploring look. "It is urgent that I see him."

Two visitors passed them on their way to the castle, startling Aislin. Her gaze darted to them, but after a moment, she released her breath, and seemed more at ease.

"I was hoping he'd turn up today," she said with a shake of her head. "I don't like that he's late. Every day he fails to turn up increases my fear that something has happened to him."

William was also worried.

His first concern was for his brother, that Aislin was right, and he'd been hurt or killed. But he also had another concern. Aislin had told him Gideon was alive and had gone to Plymouth for the militia, but what if it was an utter fabrication? If Gideon had done so, then why hadn't anyone in Plymouth recalled seeing him?

Not that she was purposely lying to him. He trusted his instincts and sensed this girl believed what she was saying. However, what if she was lying to herself? Although she appeared rational, how would he know if she wasn't?

She might have seen Gideon die.

She might have been the one to stab him and then been unable to reconcile herself to what she had done. If that were so, it would not be so farfetched for her to believe Gideon was still alive when he wasn't.

Or steal into his room last night and attempt to stab him.

And not remember anything of it today.

Bah! If she were mad, wouldn't he be able to tell?

"My lord, if he doesn't appear before I leave, will you wait for him? I have news he must be given."

"That depends."

His response surprised her. "Depends on what?"

"On what you tell me."

She shook her head, at first not understanding what he meant. Then her eyes clouded, and she frowned at him. "You don't trust me. You think I intend to betray your brother."

He ran a hand roughly through his hair. "In truth, I don't know what to think."

She already had her hand on his arm, for he'd placed it there, but her grip now tightened. "Think what you will of me, it isn't important right now. What matters is that you get this message to your brother. There is a merchant ship known as The Evening Star sailing out of Port Isaac at the turn of the tide tomorrow."

"The Earl of Exmoor's new ship? How did it come to be here?"

Her eyes rounded. "You know of it? Of him?"

He cast her a wry smile. "I'm quite familiar with all the Brayden family. We are connected by marriage. My sister is now married to Exmoor's cousin." How small the world had shrunk. His sister Abby had married Tynan Brayden, Earl of Westcliff. And Westcliff was first cousin to James Brayden, Earl of Exmoor.

He had other connections to that family from his days as a pirate himself, from those years he only knew of himself as Lucifer and sailed on The Persephone under its captain, Hugh Le Brecque. Perhaps he would tell Aislin of his adventures one day or show her the burns that had scarred his skin for life, but he did not know what the future held for them.

The question weighing upon his heart was, what to do about Aislin?

He'd come for answers to reclaim his lost years.

Once his memory returned, what then? Could he bid Aislin farewell and leave her behind? Could he trust her? Was she in possession of her wits? "What is The Evening Star doing here? It should have sailed out of Plymouth."

"A sudden squall a few days ago. It happens often enough along the St. George's Channel and the Irish Sea. It is a common trade route. Plymouth to Dublin or Drogheda, and then back down to the Continent or across the Atlantic."

"I know." His ships took those routes.

"But these squalls are dangerous," she said, sounding quite

sensible as she spoke, "so any captain with experience will sail his vessel into the closest harbor he can find. Pembroke's harbor in Wales is fairly busy and much safer since the Duke of Pembroke himself watches over the town."

"And what happens here?"

"Port Isaac's harbor is not safe. There's no one on hand to protect the ships that sail in and out. The Prince Regent has not seen fit to replace all the corrupt officials who run the port. He thinks assigning naval frigates and other ships of the line to patrol these shores is sufficient. But we know it isn't."

He didn't know a damn thing about Port Isaac, only that he'd apparently sailed into it seeking shelter from a storm and been attacked by pirates who'd destroyed his ship and left his crew, as well as himself, for dead once he'd sailed out of it.

Aislin knew who those pirates were.

Perhaps the same ones who intended to attack Exmoor's ship.

If there was any good to come out of this conversation, it was his renewed faith in Aislin. Her warning had not sounded like the deluded ravings of a madwoman. It eased his soul, for he wanted to trust her and believe in her. He also wanted to consider the possibility of something more between them. "Aislin, what else do you know that you're not telling me?"

"No, this is enough for today." She did not appear angry, nor did he sense she was trying to fool him.

"Why? What secrets are so important that you must keep them from me?"

"Secrets?" She gave a wry laugh. "My heart is an open wound because of you."

He gripped her shoulders and stared at her for a long moment. "What did I do to you back then? Did I hurt you? How?"

"You didn't hurt me." Her voice was whisper-soft and loving. "Not in the way you mean."

"Not in the way... Then how?" His hands were still on her

shoulders.

Up close, she appeared so young and innocent. She was scared, but not of him.

No, she did not fear him.

He knew women.

He knew that look.

Was it possible she loved him?

Merciful heaven! What had he done to her?

Chapter Six

"COME, MY LORD. Don't frown at me when we have so little time together. Put aside your questions for now, and let's enjoy this lovely day." Aislin left his side and started up the steps to the castle ruins. "We can sit overlooking the water and chat. I've brought us some food to share. It isn't much. I couldn't risk taking more. It would have been noticed."

"Thus putting you in danger?"

She shook her head. "No, it would have put *you* in danger."

This slender girl still thought to protect him? He studied her as they walked in silence through the ruins. She wore sturdy walking boots and a gown of pale gray muslin that matched the color of her eyes. The silk trim on her gown and the soft leather of her boots were the only signs of wealth. Of course, she spoke and carried herself like a lady.

But she had no chaperone.

She roamed as wild and free as the ponies on Bodmin Moor.

Her dark hair was unbound, just as it had been yesterday and in his dreams.

The light wind ruffled her hair and caused the long, silky strands to curl around her hips.

He wanted to bury his hands in those dark locks and run his fingers through them. He wanted to bury himself inside her, but he held that longing on a tight tether. How many other men felt the same about her?

Despite her innocence, there was an unmistakable sensuality about Aislin. In the shape of her mouth, the swell of her bosom, and the expressiveness of her eyes beneath their sooty lashes.

He settled on a patch of grass and propped his back against a low wall of stones. He sat looking out toward the sea, his arms casually resting on his bent knees, but on the inside, he was roiling with tension.

Aislin settled beside him, close enough for him to breathe in the subtle temptation of her lavender scent.

She fixed her gaze across the water, seemingly unaware of his turmoil. "I've been coming here for years. It's such a beautiful place. I often allow my dreams to take flight when I'm out here." She turned to him, a light blush on her cheeks. "There's magic in the air. In the stones. In the caves below. In the cliffs and sea. Whenever I'm here, I forget who I am."

"Aislin," he said, regretting he was about to break up their idyllic moment, "someone tried to kill me last night."

She gasped and turned to him. "William, no!" In the next moment, she realized what she'd called him and blushed furiously. "Forgive me, my lord. I shouldn't have called you that. I have no right. I... Did you get a glimpse of your assailant? Describe him to me."

"I didn't see him. I happened to be out of my room when this devil crept in. He stood over my bed, thinking he was stabbing me as I slept. But he mistook the bulge of my pillows for my body."

She gaped at him, seeming unable to speak or breathe.

"I had tucked them under my covers to make it appear I was in bed. But I had slipped out of the inn to explore the town. I never expected someone to enter my bedchamber intending to cut short my life."

The breath rushed out of her in a sob, and she buried her face in her hands. "Not even a day. It's happening again. Thank goodness you weren't there. Thank goodness he didn't hurt you. I'd never forgive myself if he had."

She was shaking and appeared so fragile in that moment, he was afraid she'd snap like a twig. He drew her into his arms to comfort her. "Aislin, I'm fine. He didn't hurt me."

What was wrong with him? She'd taken his words like a punch to the stomach, and he'd purposely blurted them in the hope of getting an unguarded response from her.

Well, he'd succeeded.

Until this very moment, she'd impressed him as having a spirit forged of steel, strong and resilient. A spirit that could never be broken.

He'd gotten it all wrong. She was hurting so badly, the pain was eating her insides. How had he missed this? She'd even mentioned it clearly, claiming her heart was an open wound. Only he hadn't been listening properly and had dismissed her comment.

More to his regret, he'd been prepared to dismiss her as a madwoman when quite the opposite was true. She was risking her life to help Gideon and was now trying to protect him.

She tried to draw away, but he wouldn't let her. "Forgive me. I'm a fool. I shouldn't have dropped the news on you like that. And you may call me William. I give you permission." It seemed a foolish thing to say. *Someone tried to kill me, but call me William if it makes you feel better.*

"William," she repeated with a bitter laugh. "They won't stop trying until they succeed. Please, you must go. Now."

"Not before I have my answers."

She resisted the tug of his arms, pushing against him when he held her back. Finally, she stopped struggling.

He took it as permission to begin questioning her. "Aislin, who else are you protecting? Other than me and Gideon?"

"I can't tell you."

"You *won't* tell me. That is not at all the same thing. Don't you realize? Your silence puts us all in greater danger. Who are you protecting?"

Tears welled in her eyes. "If I tell you, then you must promise not to go after them. They will kill you."

"Who is *they*? I want names, Aislin. Tell me everything. It is the only way to keep us alive." She'd said it was happening again. Those were her exact words. What did she mean by it?

"My lord–"

"William. I gave you permission to call me that."

She grunted in obvious irritation and shook her head. "William, then. I must ask a favor of you."

"What is it?"

"Please kiss me again." The request came in a whisper. "One kiss and I'll tell you all of it afterward."

It seemed a small sacrifice to make in order to obtain the truth, but he sensed it meant so much more.

What was she about to tell him that would create a chasm wide enough to tear them apart forever?

He tipped her chin up so that she met his gaze. He found himself looking into the saddest eyes he'd ever beheld.

Lord, he couldn't bear it. "Close your eyes, Aislin."

She obeyed.

Her lips were trembling, those beautiful lips the color of pink roses.

He closed his eyes and pressed his mouth to hers, bracing himself for the jolt he knew would rush through him the moment their lips touched. Even so, he was unprepared for the impact to his heart.

"Aislin," he murmured, swallowing her in his embrace. He wanted to take all of her in, build a wall around them that no villains could ever surmount.

But this was truly fantasy.

The villains had already broken in and tried to kill him.

He didn't care for himself, but what of Aislin? What would they do to her?

Her mouth was soft and pliant. She offered no resistance when he deepened the kiss, seeming to crave it as much as he craved her. Nor did she draw back when he slid his tongue inside her mouth to tease and tangle it with hers, for there was nothing tame about his feelings for her.

He had not lived the life of a monk. He was no stranger to the physical pleasures of a woman's body. But holding Aislin. Kissing her. Breathing in her scent. The sensations she aroused were beyond anything he'd ever felt before.

He ran his fingers through her unbound hair. It was lush and long and spun from dark silk.

Her skin, he noted as his lips moved along the slender curve of her neck, tasted of sea salt and lavender. If this was to be their last day together, he was going to take as much from her as she was willing to give.

They were alone now, no travelers wandering around to interrupt their pleasure. No carriages or horses other than theirs grazing on the nearby gorse and hedgerows. Nothing surrounding them but sky and ruins and the eternal sea. He eased her down on the grass and rolled her under him, settling his body over hers. "Aislin…"

She did not seem to mind the brazenness of their position, him atop her. She tugged on his shoulders to draw him down. He felt the soft give of her breasts against his chest.

He wanted to claim her.

She would let him.

What then?

He was not in the habit of despoiling innocents, he reminded himself.

"Damnation. I'm sorry." He sat up suddenly and shook his

head to clear away the thoughts he should not be having…or acting upon with this girl.

It took her a moment to open her eyes, but she cast him a wry smile when she saw him obviously struggling with himself. "I am almost two and twenty. Old enough to know my own mind."

Her willingness gave him no relief. "You are unmarried."

She laughed and sat up beside him. "Nor do I care if I ever marry. There is no one for me in Port Isaac or any other Cornwall town. Surely, you must know…it cannot be a surprise to you." She looked away to hide her embarrassment. "There is only you."

Were he a knave, he'd take full advantage.

"William, I love you."

The words hung in the air between them, thick and silent.

"Aislin…"

She laughed softly. "You do not need to respond. I didn't expect you to."

His heart pounded.

She was willing, and she loved him.

All the more reason he would not touch her outside of marriage. *Marriage.* Is this what he had come back here for, to take her as his wife?

To do otherwise would destroy this beautiful creature, this enchanted faerie princess. This woman of his dreams.

He could never destroy her.

She was innocent, had never experienced a man's touch or known passion. He could tell by the awkward way she'd clutched him when he'd kissed her just now. Also in the way she'd responded when he'd slipped his tongue into her mouth. At first confused and unsure. It was a new experience for her, one she'd accepted because it was *his* tongue probing her velvet depths. *His* body weighing down on her. *His* mouth grinding gently against hers.

Most women her age were married and had borne children by now.

Yet, no man had claimed Aislin.

She had been saving herself for him.

Which brought him back to the earlier question roiling in the back of his mind. What had he done to her back then? He may not have ruined her, but...she regarded him with such longing, he knew he'd done something worse.

He'd stolen her heart.

And having stolen it, no other man could ever possess it.

He took her into his arms and turned her so that she faced outward toward the sea while her back rested against his chest. He was sitting up and had once again propped his back against the low, stone wall. "Aislin, tell me the truth now," he said, trying to speak calmly as he struggled to still his thundering heart. "I give you my word, I'll protect you no matter what you tell me. What happened to me back then? More important, what is going on now?"

He felt her shudder.

She took a deep breath and began. "My name is Aislin Farnsworth. My...my...father..." She tried to continue, but her voice was shaking. She drew another breath and let it out slowly. "My father runs the Farnsworth Inn. It's in Port Isaac. But I grew up in Polzeath. He did not want me raised beside the docks."

"The inn is beside the harbor?"

"Yes. Within sight of the ships, a rough place, attracting the human sort of vermin."

She turned and lifted to her knees to stare at him, obviously waiting for him to say something.

When he didn't, she continued. "My father is known as Gentleman Jack Farnsworth. He claims to be the by-blow of an earl. I don't suppose it matters, for he'll never be accepted into good Society."

"No, he never will," William agreed, for those who regarded themselves as everyone's betters fiercely guarded their ranks. No amount of wealth would ever be enough to allow an unacknowl-edged bastard into that elevated circle.

Aislin gave a curt nod. "Nor will I ever be counted among them. Still, Jack hoped to raise me as a lady. He said I was beautiful and could make something of myself. I even had governesses and tutors at one point. Not that he doted upon me. He didn't. Whatever aspirations he had were for himself alone. I was but a means for him to achieve his goal."

"Of elevating his status?"

"Yes, but everything changed when I turned eighteen."

William frowned. "What happened?"

"I'm not sure. He went to London to arrange for my debut." She rolled her eyes and gave a mirthless laugh. "He came home with his tail between his legs. It was just as you pointed out. No amount of wealth would ever gain him the respectability he sought. Nor would any gentleman ever take me as his wife, no matter how pretty I was or how generous my dowry."

She followed the flight of a plover as it circled overhead. "He must have been humiliated. A proud man like him, used to being treated with awe and respect. In the blink of an eye, my tutors, my seamstress, and my dancing instructor were all dismissed. *You'll make yourself useful at the inn*, he said to me."

"And that's where we met? At the Farnsworth Inn in Port Isaac."

"Yes. I'd only been working there a few months before you strode in with your brother and a few of your crewmen. You'd made it safely into port just as the storm hit. I was the barmaid who served you."

She shifted uncomfortably, making no move to get off her knees. He frowned, for it seemed as though she was supplicating to him. He knew she wasn't intending to, but this was how it looked to him.

"So, you see," she said, misunderstanding his frown, "that's all I am. A girl who works at an inn, serving drinks in its taproom because men drink more when served by a pretty face."

He rose and brought her to her feet. "You are an innkeeper's daughter. There is nothing shameful in that."

She cast him a look of dismay. "No, there isn't. But that isn't all he is. Why do you think you sent Gideon off in the middle of a raging storm to fetch the Plymouth militia?" She put her hands on his chest, but he wasn't certain whether it was to draw him closer or shove him away. "Don't make me say the last of it. Can you not guess? Must you be so cruel?"

"Yes, Aislin." Because he still remembered none of it. "I will hear it from your lips."

She broke away and ran through the ruins, down the hill to where she'd tethered her horse next to his. He followed her, cursing the haze of his lost memories that refused to lift. He was forcing her to relate events that tormented her as much as they did him.

She'd reached her horse and was about to climb onto her saddle when he caught up to her. He lifted her into his arms, holding her fast so that she could not break away. "Don't fight me, Aislin."

Although he had no memory of that storm-ravaged night, it would take a simpleton not to understand what she was saying. "Your father, Gentleman Jack Farnsworth...he ordered my ship attacked. Why? We could not have been sailing with a full cargo, only a few wares to trade in Dublin or Drogheda. That's where we would have picked up our profitable cargo."

He eased his hold, not wishing to bruise her. But he was not about to let her go. If she slipped away from him this time, he knew she would never come back. "What made him choose my ship?"

"It wasn't about the goods or your vessel." She stopped resisting him, realizing it was futile. She groaned in utter misery. "He saw the way I looked at you. He knew what I felt for you, so he ordered you killed. It was *you* he went after. You didn't even know my name, and he wanted you dead. I did this to you. I was responsible for the death of your crew."

She tried to push away again, but he hugged her close instead. "Oh, Aislin. My Aislin. How can you blame yourself for what your father did?"

Her tears began to flow in earnest. "How can I not?" She gazed at him in astonishment.

"Tell me the rest of it. Did you try to warn me?"

"Of course! When I overheard him speaking to his men, forming his plan, I rushed upstairs and told you all I knew. I begged you to leave at once."

He cast her a mirthless smile. "That's why I kissed you. For risking your life to save me."

"Yes, but it doesn't matter now. Your men are dead. Your ship is lost."

She'd lived with the guilt and shame for three years. He would not allow her to blame herself a moment longer. "It isn't your fault."

He saw the raw pain in her eyes and knew that a mere conciliatory pat on the head would never release her from the burden of blame she carried. "Not your fault," he repeated, though he expected the assurance would fall on deaf ears.

What her father had done was his sin alone.

"How can you not hate me?" Aislin punctuated the question with a shudder.

Hate her? He wanted to protect this angel with his life. His heart had always remembered her. These feelings she'd aroused had never been forgotten.

Nor would they ever.

Of course, her bastard-of-a-father had just assumed he, an English baron, would use his daughter for only one thing, his sexual pleasure. Perhaps take her on as his mistress and then discard her once he'd tired of her.

The wind blew her unbound hair off her face so that he had an unobstructed view of her loveliness. Her mouth was a touch too wide. Her eyes were a shimmering, silver-gray, framed by long, dark lashes. Her lips were full and pink as roses.

"I must go now, my lord. You see why I must. How can you want anything more to do with me?"

Her only crime was to feel a stirring in her heart for him, just as he'd felt his heart stirring for her.

Had he told her how he felt back then?

Would she believe him if he told her now? "No, Aislin. We're in this together."

"In *what* together? My father tried to kill you. Go home while you still can, Lord Whitpool."

"William."

"My lord," she insisted. "Let your brother take care of the pirates who bring death and destruction in these coastal waters. You're the baron. Reclaim your life. Marry someone worthy of you, and sire sons and daughters as fine as you."

"I won't leave you to face your father's wrath alone." He put a finger to her lips when she made to protest. "My business is far from finished here."

"You have no *business* here. Be content you've found me. Now go. Please!"

He shook his head. "Not before I see Gideon again."

"But he hasn't been here in over a month. That has me very worried," she admitted. "Not for me. My father won't harm me. But what if he's gotten his hands on Gideon?"

"Then that settles it. I'm going to find him."

She gasped. "You fool! Why are you so stubborn? If Gentleman Jack Farnsworth got his hands on your brother, then he is long since dead. Your looking for him will only lead you to the same end."

"But you don't know for certain that your father has him."

"No, but..." She sighed. "Very well, we're in this together. However, I must be the one to search for him. You need to ride to Plymouth and return with the militia."

"As Gideon tried to do? Did he ever make it there? And who among the officers can I trust? No, Aislin. All I need from you is to feed me information, then go home and pretend you know nothing about me."

She rolled her eyes. "Someone tried to kill you last night. He could have been sent by my father, which means he knows you are here."

"And now he believes me dead."

"You don't know this. I may have been followed here today. His lackey will report that you're still alive."

"Do you think you were followed?"

She nibbled her lip. "I don't know. I didn't notice anyone on my trail, but the man might be more cautious than I give him credit for."

"Seems to me your father and his men have grown too bold. Had he sent a man after you, he would have meant for you to see him."

She frowned. "Perhaps."

"Not perhaps. If he thinks I'm dead, then he'd want you to know that he killed me." He sighed and ran a hand through his hair. "But this would leave me free to search for Gideon while your father's guard is down."

"No! I will search for you."

"Aislin–"

"He won't have reason to guard himself if he no longer feels threatened by you. Besides, you wouldn't know where to start."

William gripped her shoulders, wanting to shake sense into her. "And you would?"

She nodded. "Better than you, my lord. I will talk to his men. I will talk him into confessing, perhaps. Men loosen their tongues when they've been drinking. They boast to impress a pretty woman."

She blushed, obviously uncomfortable with thinking of herself as that. But beauty such as hers would never go unnoticed by men. It wouldn't matter what sort. Gentlemen. Scum. They'd all look their fill.

They'd all desire to possess her.

Hadn't he desired just this thing?

"The more I think on it," she continued, "if Gideon has come to harm, then it couldn't have been by my father's hand. You're right. He would not have kept quiet about your brother's death. He would have taunted me with the news, boasted to me of it, for that is his way. So, it is more likely your brother is hurt. Or he's been killed by someone else's hand. Either way, I'm the best hope you have of finding out what happened to him."

He cast her an angry look. "I don't want you involved."

She laughed. "Too late for that. Three years too late. Let's review all we know. Tell me about Gideon. Was he a resourceful boy? Did he have a favorite hiding spot? Somewhere he would go to lick his wounds if he were angry or injured?"

"How is it relevant to what he might do now?"

"Do people change? My governess was one of the cleverest women I'd ever met. She used to tell me that a person's nature stays with them throughout their lives. A sweet and noble child becomes a sweet and noble adult. An intolerant and temperamental child–"

"Becomes an intolerant and temperamental adult?"

She nodded. "I'm hoping Gideon was a resourceful, clever child."

William managed a smile. "He was."

"So, you see, it is important we think like him. If he were injured, where would he hide?"

William's heart beat a little faster, for the girl made sense. "I don't know this area, other than in my dreams." *Those damn dreams.* "But you were raised here. You know the terrain. You know the rhythm of the waves and the moon tides. You know these towns and the pirates who control them. More important, you know the magistrates and harbor masters who are in the pocket of these fiends."

She nodded. "I do. This is why I must return to Port Isaac and pretend nothing has happened. Let me find out what I can from my father and his men. I'll ask at the local gaol, as well. But you must promise to stay out of Port Isaac. Stay here a while longer…as long as you can today. I keep hoping Gideon will appear. If he does, give him the message about Exmoor's ship and then leave."

"Leave? No, Aislin. Nor can I promise to stay out of Port Isaac." The soft gray of her eyes turned to fiery embers, blazing at him. He knew he was being stubborn, and she was afraid for his life. "But I will be careful."

He'd be shot the moment he entered the Farnsworth Inn. Perhaps the moment he stepped foot in Port Isaac. But only if he was recognized.

"I'll meet you back here in two days' time," she said with a reluctant nod. "Do not attempt anything foolish. Think about where your brother might hide. You came here with a driver. Mr. Musgrove? He's a local man and trusted in these parts. Let him come to me at the tavern if you've found out anything important."

She was being logical and cautious, but he didn't like the thought of being away from her even for a day. He meant to suggest another plan, but a glint of metallic light suddenly caught his eye. The horses began to neigh and grow skittish.

He grabbed Aislin and pulled her down with him behind one of the stone walls just as a shot rang out. "Stay here. I'm going after him."

"William, no!"

But he'd already withdrawn a pistol from his boot and left her side to chase after the assailant.

Was it the same man who'd tried to kill him last night?

Was he trying to finish the job he'd botched?

Or had Aislin been his intended target?

Chapter Seven

A ISLIN WANTED TO chase after William but understood this was the worst thing she could do. Then she realized she could not run after him even if she wished it. Pain ripped through her. She felt a burn along her thigh and the ooze of warm liquid through her gown, soaking the fabric.

She put a hand to her leg. Blood trickled through her fingers, leaving a crimson stain on her hand.

She gasped.

The blackguard had shot her, the ball tearing clean through her flesh. Fortunately, it hadn't lodged in the muscle or bone.

Still, it hurt like blazes.

She tried to rip her chemise to fashion a bandage for herself but could not manage it. Her hands were shaking too badly, and she seemed to be losing strength.

"William," she whispered, wishing him back to her side. But she knew it was more important for him to catch the assailant.

Had the man purposely aimed at her? If so, it couldn't have been one of her father's men. Gentleman Jack Farnsworth, for all his faults, loved her in his own distorted way.

Perhaps love wasn't the proper word. She was his daughter, his treasured possession, and he would never sink so low as to damage any of his valuables, certainly never his only child.

Which left the question, who wanted her dead?

Or had the man meant to shoot William and missed?

It felt like hours but could only have been a few minutes before William returned. He took one look at the red stain on her gown and fell to his knees beside her. "Aislin!"

"I'm all right." But her voice was shaking and so was her body. "I need to bind my leg. I couldn't manage it on my own. You'll have to do it. Use my chemise."

She'd seen him draw a pistol from one of his boots.

She laughed softly as he now withdrew a knife from the other. "You came prepared, didn't you?"

He cast her a tender but mirthless smile as he made quick work of cutting the delicate fabric into a long, white strip and securing it to the wound. "I'll get you to a doctor. I heard there is a good one in Trevena."

He glanced over his shoulder to the town that could be seen from the ruins.

"Yes, Dr. Jones. Take me to his infirmary and leave me there. He can send word to my father." She studied him as he bound her wound, noting the grind of his teeth and clench of his jaw as a mark of his tension.

She sighed, not up to battling him right now. But she knew he did not wish to leave her side. The stubborn man would make a fuss loud enough to alert everyone in the village of Trevena. Someone would scurry off to report to her father and make an easy coin, for Gentleman Jack always rewarded those who carried news to him.

For William's sake, her father could not find them together or ever find out they'd been together. "William, did you catch him?"

"No, love."

She closed her eyes and swallowed hard. Had he meant to use this endearment? Probably only to soothe her. He couldn't possibly love her, this beautiful, big man with golden hair and emerald eyes and a body as powerful as any knight of legend. "Do you think he was aiming at you? Or me? Perhaps he only meant to scare us and accidentally shot me."

He ran a hand through his hair and frowned. "I don't know. More damn questions and still no answers."

She placed a hand on his arm for no reason other than she needed to hold on to him. "If he shot me on purpose, then he couldn't have been my father's man. No matter how dangerous Jack Farnsworth is, I'm still his daughter. In his twisted mind, the evil he did to you was to protect me."

"I'm taking you back to Boscastle with me."

She rolled her eyes in frustration. Were all barons this irritating? "No! Are you not listening? If I don't return to Port Isaac, my father will come looking for me."

"Let him. His distraction will work in our favor. Perhaps in favor of the Crown as well, by drawing him out of his stronghold. It might also keep him from sailing after Exmoor's ship. This doctor in Trevena, how good is he?"

"I'm not sure. I've never needed him before, but he has an excellent reputation. And come to think of it, he might know something about your brother. Trevena is close enough to the castle, and he's often out on the road to see one patient or another. He might have noticed something the day Gideon disappeared. I'll ask him."

"No, I'll do it."

"If I had a cudgel, I'd beat you about the ears."

Despite the seriousness of their situation, he chuckled. "Is this any way to speak to a baron?"

She couldn't help but return his smile. "Yes, if he's as stubborn and infuriating as you are. No one here will speak to you. But they'll confide in me."

"Even this doctor? How well do you know him?"

"Not very," she admitted. "As I said, I've haven't had need of him before. He's come to my father's inn often enough. There's always trouble in the taproom. Drunken sailors are always brawling. The point is, we're all familiar with each other in the area. He won't consider me a stranger. But you? His mouth will be sealed tighter than a clamshell."

William did not look pleased, nor did he appear swayed by her logic. "Aislin, you're hurt. I can't simply leave you in the doctor's care and trust he'll get you safely back to Port Isaac. What do you think your father will do when he sees you limp back in this condition? He'll question everyone until he finds out what happened. Then he'll tear through these towns in a rage. Let me take you back to Boscastle after the doctor treats your wound. We'll work out what to do then."

"And where am I to stay?" She arched an eyebrow. "With you?"

He sighed in obvious frustration. "I'll inquire about obtaining a separate room."

"I may not be a fine lady, but I still have my good name to consider. My reputation will be in tatters if word spreads that I stayed with you. My father will be even more enraged."

"I'd rather he aimed his fury at me alone. And didn't I just say I'd get you separate lodgings?"

"The Pendragon Inn is a reputable establishment. An unmarried young lady cannot stay there without a chaperone."

"Then I'll ask one of the local women to attend you."

"And then what? Have them put me in a room as far away from you as possible? Where anyone can get at me? You wouldn't hear my screams, assuming I am even able to scream while this villain chokes me."

"I can't believe you are fighting me on this. You ride from Port Isaac to Tintagel Castle on your own, spend hours roaming the countryside without escort every day. You roam as wild and free as the ponies on Bodmin Moor, and you're squawking about this?" He ran a hand through his hair again and groaned. "I'll have them put you in a room next door to mine."

She understood his concern, but his suggestion would never do. "That is as bad as putting me in *your* room. You know it won't work."

"We'll make it work. You are injured. I'm not leaving your side."

This man was stubborn and caring but taking her to Boscastle was a mistake. "No matter which room I'm in, you'll insist on sitting up to watch over me through the night. This is your nature, to control things."

"I'd rather think of myself as protective." He laughed bitterly. "Nothing has been in my control for the last three years."

"Your memory will come back in time, just as my leg will mend given time. It is but a graze."

"It's far more serious than that, and the assailant may try again."

"He won't dare while I am under my father's protection. My lord, what you suggest is out of the question. It is folly."

He caressed her cheek, running his knuckles gently across her cool skin. "Everything I've done up to now is folly. I've dreamed of you. Searched for you. I've kissed you…more than once. Three times now if we are counting from back when we first met."

She wanted to cry, for those kisses had meant everything to her. "How does a kiss change anything?"

"Three kisses," he insisted. "Aislin, you're hurt. I know what you say makes sense, but I cannot leave you. It's as simple as that. I will not do it. If you're concerned about the impropriety, then I'll do the honorable thing. You needn't worry."

She laughed. No, he could not possibly be thinking… "And what is this honorable thing you have in mind?"

"To marry you, of course."

Quite the oddest sensation fell over her. Her body grew warm, and tingles began to shoot throughout her limbs. Her heart soared.

She loved this man who had the power to so easily break her heart. "You are mad, my lord. Take me to the doctor. We'll figure out the rest afterward."

"Aislin…"

"We must go. You chased the bounder off, but what's to stop him from returning to finish the job?"

He lifted her into his arms.

Aislin could not stop staring at William as he carried her to the horses. Nor could she keep her heart from aching for him. That he still spoke to her, that he still looked at her without disgust, was incomprehensible to her. She loved him and had admitted it to him, but how could he possibly feel anything other than revulsion for her?

She glanced at the village of Trevena, so quiet and peaceful in the distance.

He cast her a stubborn look when they reached the field of gorse where the horses were tethered. "You'll ride with me."

It wasn't a question or a request.

He lifted her onto his saddle and then climbed up behind her. She heard the steady beat of his heart, felt the heat of his big body against her back as he wrapped his arms around her and drew her firmly against his chest.

She leaned her head upon his shoulder.

"How do you feel, love?"

Wonderful despite her pain and nausea.

He'd said it again. *Love.*

She nestled in his arms, surrounded herself with his strength, and absorbed his musk scent and the maleness of him. He was gentle with her. She felt protected. "I'm fine, William."

He led her mount by the reins, not that he had to, for her sweet mare would have followed her anywhere. "Aislin, how do you really feel?"

She supposed her shivers gave her away.

She felt dizzy. Weak. She must have lost more blood than she realized. "I'm in your arms. There's no better place to be. I'm fine, really."

"Why do I not believe you?"

WILLIAM STOOD IN the examination room of the Trevena doctor's infirmary, holding Aislin's hand while the man treated her wound. She'd introduced him as Hamish Jones, a Welshman if he ever saw one, for he had dark hair and dark eyes and a rugged look about him. Not to mention the Welsh accent that stood out even though he obviously tried to hide it.

What was the doctor doing in Cornwall?

He supposed it did not matter. Men had their reasons for leaving home and never returning.

William gazed out the window to stare at the row of trim, whitewashed houses with colorful shutters that stood across the road from the infirmary. His heart was racing, but he tried to will himself to calmness as the doctor patched Aislin's leg.

Someone had shot his Aislin.

Yes, *his* Aislin.

He was going to marry her, even if they had to run off like desperate young lovers to Gretna Green to do it.

But first, he was going to find the culprit who did this to her and rip him apart with his bare hands.

Aislin was in obvious pain, but he could do nothing about it other than hold her hand and mouth meaningless platitudes.

As the minutes wore on, he could no longer bear to stand by and watch her suffer. Her injury tore at his soul. She was in agony and purposely trying to be strong for him, forcing herself to hold back her tears and smother her cries of pain.

Since his presence was only making things more difficult for her, he muttered an excuse to slip out of the examination room. After taking a quick turn outside the infirmary to make certain no one had followed them, he returned to stand in the waiting room.

But this proved worse for him.

He began to pace like a caged lion.

"My lord, you will wear a hole through the floorboards," Aislin teased a short while later, struggling to walk toward him.

He'd been so preoccupied, his gut so twisted in knots over her injury, he hadn't realized the doctor had finished treating her. She was holding on to the man's arm for assistance. Her face was pale and her features drawn.

She limped toward him, trying her best to hide her discomfort, but she winced with every step, and even the slightest movement made her blanche. However, she held her chin up and did not shirk from his steady gaze.

Ah, yes. This was Aislin, his proud Celtic princess. Ever stubborn and determined to overcome all obstacles.

The look on her face brought relief to his heart, but he could not manage a smile. Her injury was too serious to dismiss. However, she had spirit. She was a fighter and would do all in her power to keep up with him because she wanted so badly to protect him as she had three years ago. "My lord, you must listen to what Dr. Jones has to say."

He arched an eyebrow and studied the man who now held his Aislin.

His Aislin.

Yes, she is my Aislin.

He could not imagine going through life without her.

The doctor appeared to be about ten years older than William, of average height, and slight in build. However, there was an unmistakable harshness in the curve of his mouth and a resentment in his eyes that William found surprising. Doctors were healers, but this man looked haunted, almost feral. Like a hunted animal.

A wounded, hunted animal.

He sighed.

He'd rarely seen such a look on any man, even in the midst of battle. But who was to say what anyone ought to look like? Aislin was the perfect example, a pirate's daughter who looked like an angel. Dr. Jones might have had a hard upbringing. He must have had reason to run from his Welsh home. That he'd turned to healing others in order to ease his own torment spoke well of his character.

Still, it was a flawed character.

"You are Gideon Croft's brother?"

Although William had not taken particular care to hide his identity, he did not expect the man's first words to be this question. What did he know of Gideon? Or his whereabouts? "I am. Why do you ask?"

Aislin slipped from the doctor's grasp and came to William's side, now placing her hand on his arm. It was to comfort him, for she knew the doctor's words had unsettled him. He wanted to kiss her for it. "Gideon's been shot, but it wasn't my father's doing."

Perhaps it was the same assailant who'd injured Aislin. He glanced from Aislin to the doctor. "Shot? How do you know? Have you seen him?"

"Not in some time," the doctor replied, "but I think I know who did it. A rogue agent for the Crown lured your brother into an ambush. I'm an agent as well. Unfortunately, there is a traitor in our midst."

"Dr. Jones, I'm afraid you have me at a disadvantage. I know nothing of the espionage going on around here." How could he be sure it wasn't the doctor himself who'd shot his brother? Assuming any of what he'd just said was true. Dear heaven, what had Aislin told the man? "Where is Gideon now? Is he alive?"

William thought it was safer to play along for now, pretend to believe him.

His pistol was loaded and in easy reach. His knife was also close at hand.

"I hope he is alive. I believe he is. I found him lying injured by Tintagel Castle and brought him here to treat his wounds. He was rambling and mostly incoherent. He ran a high fever for several days. Then one night, he disappeared from my infirmary. There was no sign of foul play, so I suspect he ran off on his own. Or rather, stumbled off. He wasn't well. I searched for him. He couldn't have gotten far, but I haven't seen him since."

William said nothing, trying to absorb the news and decide whether to trust this man or not. It all sounded like nonsense to him.

"I thought perhaps he'd contacted you, my lord. That you'd come here at his urging."

"No, he hasn't. I came here only to find Miss Farnsworth. Until my arrival a few days ago, I had no idea my brother was alive. It eases my heart greatly to know he is, but if he's on assignment for the Crown, then it is not my place to interfere. My only intention right now is to return home and bring Miss Farnsworth back with me…as my wife."

Aislin pursed her lips, those beautiful lips he ached to kiss. "Ignore him, Dr. Jones. He is not thinking clearly."

The doctor arched an eyebrow and grinned. "He appears to be a man on a mission, and I cannot find fault with his plan."

"There is no plan. I have no intention of returning with him to London." She scowled at William. "If there is a traitor in our midst, it is possible my father will know his identity."

"Do you think this man would be in touch with your father?" William asked.

"It doesn't matter whether he is or not. Gentleman Jack Farnsworth knows everyone. He pays to know everything going on around him. Do you think he would ever allow another Cornwall pirate to harm me? When he learns of what happened to me, he will destroy this villain and anyone harboring him. So you see, my lord, I must return to Port Isaac. I'll tell my father what has happened and then cajole as much information as I can out of him. I'll relay it to Dr. Jones when he comes to tend me. In turn, he will relay it to you."

Her expression softened, and although she was trying to appear strong, he saw that she was trembling. "Aislin–"

"Dr. Jones found Gideon in one of the caves below Tintagel Castle. Gideon had been shot on the beach but managed to crawl into the cave. Not that it would have done him much good, for the tide fills the caves. Another half hour, and it would have become his watery grave. As the tide ebbed, his body would have been swept out to sea."

"It is true, my lord." The doctor ran a hand through his mane of dark hair. "I carried him to my infirmary, hid him here, and then started the rumor he'd drowned. No doubt the traitor assumed this is precisely what had happened, his body swallowed up in the vast expanse. I did not tell the other agents that it was a ruse. I allowed them to believe Gideon was dead. I'm the only one who knows he is alive…well, hopefully still alive."

William tried to steady the rampant beat of his heart before it pounded a hole through his chest. He had been walking in the ruins above where Gideon had lain injured only a few weeks ago. Where was his brother now?

The doctor cleared his throat. "I'm telling you this because…it is possible he will return to the cave tonight."

William arched an eyebrow. "Why would he do this?"

"His injuries haven't healed properly. We used to arrange meetings there on the night of the full moon. He might return, even if only to allow me to treat him. You are his brother. Only you can persuade him to leave Cornwall. Get him away from here. His work is done."

"And what of you, Dr. Jones? Did he reveal the identity of the traitor to you? Surely, he would have said something during his delusional rambling."

"No, he didn't." The doctor shrugged. "So, we must go on as we have before. Waiting for this traitor to make a mistake. I don't know. I may be next on this man's list. He may believe I know his identity and am merely playing coy. It is a risk I am willing to take."

"For the good of the Crown?"

He cast William a wry smile. "Do you not trust that a Welshman can be loyal? We are not all rebels."

"Forgive me, Doctor. I did not wish to sound ungrateful for all you've done for my brother and Aislin." Although he could not rule him out as the villain who'd tried to kill them.

"I would not call you ungrateful, my lord. Perhaps cynical as to my motives. Let me assure you, they are honorable. We have pirates in Wales as well. They are a scourge and must be wiped out. We know who most of the Cornish pirates are now. We've known for quite some time, for they've grown bold and no longer fear the authorities."

"Most of those in authority are in the pocket of these scoundrels," Aislin added, making a moue of disgust. "Looking the other way as they plunder despite knowing the harm they do."

"We'll round them up soon," the doctor assured. "But not before we root out those who are more dangerous to the Crown. We have enough proof to bring charges against these lower level magistrates and local militia officers who turn a blind eye to their actions. But the Crown is most concerned with this traitor. All we know is that he's high up in our ranks and giving away valuable information on all our operations in Cornwall. This one rogue agent puts all of us at risk by selling his knowledge to the highest bidder. We must discover his identity before we close in on the others."

In truth, this made little sense to William. Whoever was in charge of this operation had it backward. If the choice were his to make, he'd round up all the low-level magistrates and officers, and at the same time, bring the militia down on the pirates to round them up. Once all were in custody, what could this rogue agent do but run? It wouldn't take long to question those detained and get the truth out of them.

Offers of leniency had a way of loosening a man's tongue. The worse their crime, the faster they'd talk.

Even Gentleman Jack, as ruthless as he was, would be among the first to strike a bargain to save his own hide.

"Gideon must know who this rogue agent is. That's why he was shot," Aislin said, still holding on to William.

He put his arm around her, for she was unsteady on her feet. "Sit down, Aislin."

She obeyed him without protest, taking a seat on the lone bench that looked as thin and worn as the patients who came to the infirmary.

Damn, she was hurting worse than she let on.

He remained beside her but turned to speak to the doctor. "As for my brother, how badly was he hurt?"

"Very bad, my lord. The shot missed his heart by a hair's breadth. I'll take you to the cave with me tonight, if you wish. I'm hoping he'll turn up. He won't listen to me, of course. But together we might convince him to go home with you. Or get him to reveal the identity of the traitor."

"Assuming he shows up."

The doctor nodded. "Indeed. It may all come to naught. But do you have a better plan for finding him?"

Aislin shot him a pleading look.

What was she trying to tell him? Trust the doctor? Or don't? These past years had turned William hard. He trusted no one, had not even trusted Aislin until less than an hour ago when she'd been shot.

Indeed, these years of lost memories had changed him, and not for the better.

Perhaps Aislin would heal him in time.

Despite all the doubts and warnings about her, his heart had never wavered. He'd sought her out in his dreams. He'd come across England to find her. He'd wanted to protect her even while he worried she might kill him.

But he knew now that she would never hurt him.

He was in her soul as much as she was in his.

He shook his head in dismissal of those thoughts. He needed to concentrate his attention on the doctor. His convenient mention of Gideon, a cave, and a rendezvous on the night of a full moon all sounded like nonsense.

Still, had anything made sense this entire trip?

"What will you do?" Aislin asked, her voice alarmingly frail.

"Go to the cave, of course."

She nodded. "While I ride home and do my part."

William shook his head and groaned. "Look at yourself, Aislin. You're too weak to stand on your own much less make it to the door. No, stay right here. I'll come back for you after our visit to the cave."

"Hopefully with Gideon," she muttered.

"It is my greatest wish." He took her hands in his. "But no matter what happens, know that I will *always* come back for you."

Mother in heaven.

How had he ever suspected her of harming Gideon? Or of attempting to harm him?

He wanted to ride off with her right now, back to London, and away from Cornwall. But how could he? Her face was an alarming shade of ashen. A powdery, grayish-white that no one's skin should ever look like. Her eyes appeared glazed, and she was listing like a ship about to upend in the water.

Damn it. He thought she might faint.

"Aislin, please stay here. Wait for me. I need you to remain safely out of the way."

If the doctor proved to be the traitor, William did not want their confrontation to be anywhere near her. It would take nothing for the man to put a knife to her throat and hold her hostage.

If there was to be a fight, better to have it take place in the cave beneath Tintagel Castle. If William had to kill the doctor, he preferred to do it out of Aislin's sight.

She thought he was wonderful and heroic, a knight from the legends of Camelot. But he wasn't. He'd turned as cold and ruthless as Gentleman Jack. The only difference was, he'd never harm an innocent.

But shoot a traitor? He'd do it without blinking an eye and feel no remorse for it afterward.

Aislin was frowning at him again. "My lord–"

"You are not returning to Port Isaac."

"How do you know this is what I intended to ask?"

"Isn't it?" He knelt beside her and took her hand in his. It was cold and trembling. Not from fear, for the girl was fearless. Her wound. She'd lost too much blood.

A little color sprang into her pale cheeks. "Yes, it is. But you could not have known it."

Yes, he could. He'd been dreaming of her for years, those dreams so constant lately, they'd driven him here. He knew her mind. He knew her heart.

He knew the sweetness of her lips.

Once they were married, he'd claim her body.

But her desire to return to Port Isaac troubled him. Not that he worried for a moment she would ever betray him to her father. This need to return was a sign of her want to protect her father. As much as she loathed him for the pirate he was, she loved him as his daughter. "Your father will ask a thousand questions the moment he sees you limping. You cannot return to the Farnsworth Inn. And what will you tell him? That I was at Tintagel Castle with you?"

"No! He needn't know."

"But he will find out." The man already hated him enough to destroy his ship and all the innocent souls on it three years ago. Why would Gentleman Jack listen to reason now? "He'll use you as a lure to trap me. I don't care for myself, but I will not allow him to put you in harm's way."

"He won't."

"I'm not willing to risk it. If you are involved, and I am wounded or killed, then you will blame yourself for something that is still not your fault." He kissed her lightly on the forehead. "I would not have you put through this torment again."

The doctor eyed them both curiously.

William did not like the way this man was looking at Aislin.

Of course, he'd been a fool to kiss her. Even if it was a tame kiss on her brow. He'd also revealed his intention to marry her. "Aislin, we have time before the moon rise. Perhaps I will take you to Boscastle, after all." It wasn't perfect, but she'd be safer at the Pendragon Inn with the Sloanes and Mr. Musgrove to watch over her.

"Are you not listening to me?" Her huff of exasperation was unmistakably strong.

"I am, but I'm choosing to ignore you. Can you not see your situation? If you care nothing for your safety, then think of mine. My mind must be clear, and it won't be if I am worried about you."

"No need for the both of you to bicker about Port Isaac or Boscastle. Stay here, Miss Farnsworth, as originally suggested," the doctor said, sounding quite amiable. "I'll give you a sleeping draught to ease your pain while his lordship and I go in search of his brother."

It was not what William wanted. He did not trust the doctor. In truth, he trusted no one in Cornwall, not even the Sloane family or Mr. Musgrove. But the doctor, least of all. There were so many holes in his story. If Gideon knew the identity of the traitor, then why did he choose to run off and not reveal it to this man who was supposedly a healer and an agent for the Crown?

Nor did he trust his explanation that Gideon had been delirious and rambling until suddenly finding the wherewithal to grab his clothes and disappear into the night. And yet, despite running off, Gideon was going to conveniently return to the cave at Tintagel Castle on the night of the full moon?

This was a trap; one he was willing to walk into because he needed to know what had happened to his brother.

Would William find his bones in the cave?

The doctor cast Aislin an indulgent smile. "I've seen you walking along the cliffside at Tintagel Castle. You seemed to be waiting for someone. You came almost every day, especially these past few weeks. I knew you were waiting for Gideon."

Aislin nodded.

"Well, I think his lordship is correct. You must stay out of the way if there's to be trouble. Do not return to Port Isaac. I'll take his lordship to the cave where I found his brother. After that, we can all discuss what to do next."

William smothered the twinge of jealousy when the doctor held out his arm to Aislin, and she did not hesitate to take it. "Come, Miss Farnsworth. I've lowered the shade on the infirmary door to let everyone know I'm closed for the day. Go back in the examination room and rest. You won't be disturbed. You're looking very pale. Your leg must be on fire."

"It is."

William's heart tugged. She sounded so weak; he was almost afraid to leave her tonight.

"I'll give you something to dull the pain," the doctor said before turning to William. "I had to put in quite a few stitches. The ball tore through too much of her leg to simply bandage it. She's also lost a fair amount of blood."

Aislin lightly touched William's arm. "I wish I could go with you this evening."

He laughed in exasperation. Lord, she was a stubborn girl. "Out of the question."

She cast him a wan smile. "I'll take that as a maybe."

"It's a no."

"You'll be safer here," the doctor said. "There are too many steps to climb, my dear. You're in no condition to be scampering about those slippery rocks with your leg in its present condition."

To William's surprise, she made no further protest. "Very well, I'll stay."

His heart leapt into his throat.

Why did he not believe her?

Chapter Eight

"W ILLIAM," AISLIN SAID in a foggy whisper, trying to sit up, but only managing to prop herself on one elbow.

"What is it, love?" He'd walked into the doctor's examination room to look in on her before the doctor led him to the caves below Tintagel Castle. He dreaded what he might find.

The moon was full, a gigantic silver ball against the night sky. Stars shone brightly across the heavens.

He'd never seen such a sky in London.

However, it was a common enough sight on the sea whenever the fog wasn't hovering, which it often was.

"Do you have a pistol to spare?"

Her eyes suddenly looked clear and sharp. "Aislin, what did you do with the medicine Dr. Jones gave you to drink?"

"I tossed it out the window when he wasn't looking. Please, don't tell him, William. It smelled vile. Besides, I don't want to be asleep if anything happens."

"Promise me you won't follow us down the clifftops to the caves."

She snapped her mouth shut and tossed him a glower that would have had him laughing were this business not so serious. "Give me one of your pistols," she said, reaching out her hand.

He sighed, but after a moment's hesitation, nodded. "Very

well." After all, she'd survived the last three years using her wits. She'd been doing dangerous work, helping Gideon bring down the pirates she thought had killed him.

He removed the pistol he kept tucked in the small of his back, hidden in a fitted holster within his jacket. Although he took care to dress in the fashion of a gentleman, trim vest, Savile Row shirt, silk cravat, buff breeches, and jacket of superfine, there were sheathes and holsters tucked everywhere in his boots and garments to hide his weapons.

Villains underestimated him despite his size and trimness of his body, believing him to be a London dandy. He wasn't. He was angry as blazes and eager to rip this unknown traitor limb from limb. Then he'd start on Gentleman Jack.

"Do you know how to use it?" he muttered, handing over the weapon.

She nodded. "Trained since I was six years old. I was reliably hitting targets by the time I was seven."

He hoped she wasn't handing him a pile of hogswallop. But he saw the way she handled the pistol, weighing it in her palm, balancing it. Aiming it with proper care. "It'll do," she muttered.

He bent toward her and kissed her on the lips. "You have only the one shot. If you must use it, make it count."

She tucked the weapon in the folds of her skirt, and then eased back and closed her eyes so that she appeared to be sleeping by the time the doctor joined them. "She ought to sleep through the night," the doctor whispered, not wishing to disturb her. "We must be off before the tide comes in."

"Very well. After you, Doctor." William wondered again whether he could trust this man. He'd claimed to be working with other agents of the Crown. Of course, it stood to reason several of them would be active in the area. But where exactly?

And which of them could be trusted?

They walked under cover of night toward the ruins that ought to have looked gloomy but somehow managed to maintain their majestic splendor as moonlight spilled across the fragile stone towers and onto the water, creating a shimmering path upon the sea.

Faeries would dance upon such waters.

William silently chided himself for allowing his thoughts to wander. He forced his mind to the task at hand. Find Gideon. He didn't care how ill his brother was. If he couldn't walk out of the cave on his own two feet, William would carry him.

Assuming he was there.

Likely, he was not.

His heart lurched.

Perhaps all he'd find were Gideon's bones.

He shook off the sudden chill that ran through him.

William had been up and down these steps recently enough to remember the steep parts, which stones were loose, and the way they'd curved down to the water below. The moon's glow helped outline the castle and steps, but their path was still dangerously unlit, and the slightest misstep would send him tumbling.

He felt some relief that the doctor led the way.

He did not want the man to walk behind him, for out here it would take merely a push at just the right spot to send him falling to his death.

Since the tide was out, there was no roar of water rushing into the caves. Indeed, the soft lap of water against the beach sounded odd to his ears. It was a soothing sound, the gentle *shush, shush* of waves ebbing and flowing upon the sand.

Were circumstances different, he would bring Aislin here and make love to her under the stars. But this was yet another fanciful notion. Aislin would give herself to him, he knew. But she would not marry him.

And he would not have her outside of marriage.

He ached to have her, of course. But he would not accept anything less than to have her as his wife.

"Doctor," he whispered. "Which cave?"

"That one."

He pointed to the largest opening in the rock, one resembling the mouth of a dragon.

They'd brought torches with them, unlit while they were out in the open. But they'd have to light them now to make their way through the cave. After no more than three steps inside, they'd be plunged into an ink-black darkness.

William blinked to accustom his eyes to the sudden burst of flame as he and the doctor lit their torches. There were small pools of water on the uneven rock floor. The reds and golds of their torchlight reflected upon the water, giving the cave an ethereal glow.

He looked around.

The cave was big and dank, filled with the scent of salt water, algae, and moss.

The air was cool, almost frigid despite the heat of the day.

And yet, one could imagine Merlin down here, his sorcerer's robes long and flowing as he raised his arms and uttered an incantation to wake his sleeping dragons.

The doctor settled himself on one of the flat rocks not far from the entrance of the cave. "Now, we wait. Make yourself comfortable, my lord. We may be here for a while."

William sat on another of the flat rocks near the doctor, but also where he could keep an eye on the man as well as the cave opening. He made no effort to be discreet about his distrust. He would not let the man get behind him.

"How long before the tide comes in?" William asked, expecting that if this Welshman were the traitor, he'd make his move once the water began to rush into the cave.

"About two hours. If your brother is here, he'll make his presence known before then."

"Hmm." Gad, it all sounded like stuff and nonsense. Why had he left Aislin alone? He'd given her a pistol, but it was only capable of one shot. What if she faced two assailants?

But who would dare harm her?

She was Gentleman Jack Farnsworth's daughter.

A man would have to be insane to hurt her...and yet, someone had.

No, it had to be an errant shot, meant for him. Not her.

Still, he would not stop worrying until he had Aislin back in his arms.

He shifted uncomfortably upon the rock. They sat in silence for much of the hour, neither one caring to speak. Then suddenly, William felt a slight change to the air, and the short hairs at the nape of his neck began to stand on end.

Was it Gideon?

He rose, pistol in hand.

The doctor rose along with him and signaled for William to keep quiet. He frowned back at the man. Whoever this new arrival was, he'd know others were here because of the torchlight.

The man stepped closer.

William recognized the familiar face. Not Gideon.

"Good evening, Mr. Worthington." It was the gentleman from the room across the hall from his at the Pendragon Inn. "I'm surprised to see you here. Then again, I suppose you're surprised to find me alive."

His laugh was harsh. "You are like a cat with nine lives, my lord."

"I hope not to use them up this evening." He glanced from one man to the other. The doctor now had a pistol trained on him. William silently chided himself. He'd been sailing the seas as a privateer the past few years, and yet he'd forgotten all he'd learned.

Don't trust a stranger.

Kill him before he kills you.

At the very least, he ought to have knocked the doctor unconscious when he'd had the chance. Then it would have been one-on-one, him against Worthington. Much better odds, especially now that both men had their pistols leveled on him.

"You should not have returned to Cornwall, Lord Whitpool. Lower your weapon, if you please."

"I'm afraid I cannot. If either of you fires at me, I will get one of you, at least. But I'm certain we can reach some accommodation." William did not bat an eyelash. "Who are you really, Mr. Worthington? And what have you done with my brother? Will you do me the favor of telling me what has happened to him? I'm going to die by your hand in another moment. Where's the harm in revealing how you killed him?"

The man shrugged. "Why not?"

Ah, the hubris of such men.

Under torchlight, Worthington's haughtiness and vanity were clearly evident. He held himself above everyone, even the monarchy. "I am the Marquis of Hawley. Heir to the Duke of Exeter. Do you know him, Whitpool?"

"I'm afraid not. When in London, I generally avoided the *ton* elite." He spoke casually, as though engaged in conversation at his club. But he was going to kill this man for what he did to Aislin. He'd avenge Gideon, as well.

"The duke is my uncle. A tight-fisted, old badger. Keeps a firm grip on his purse strings. Keeps an even tighter grip on mine."

William nodded. "Alas, I see your problem. You have an appetite for the finer things in life, and Exeter has no intention of cocking up his toes any time soon."

"You do understand. I was forced to sell secrets to keep my pockets full. Harmless ones, at first."

William arched an eyebrow. "That's how it starts, doesn't it? Then before you know it, you're in too deep." He turned to glance at the doctor. "Then, you hit a complication. Dr. Jones learned of your identity. But he is also greedy and will keep silent for a price. Or was it Gideon who suspected you first?"

"Do go on, Whitpool. You seem to have it all figured out."

"Gideon realized the two of you were in collusion. That's why he slipped away from the infirmary. Or was he ever there, Doctor? I expect it is all a lie. If he knew the traitor's identity, which I suspect he did, you wouldn't have risked bringing him to your infirmary or even bothered to mend his wound. You would have killed him in the cave knowing his body would soon be swept out to sea. Are his bones here? Is this why you've brought me down here, so I will die beside my brother?"

"It does me no pleasure to harm you," the doctor said, taking a step back as a wave washed in almost far enough to break over his boots. "Nor did I wish to harm Gideon."

"Which of you shot my brother?"

Hawley sneered at him. "I did, of course. One shot through the chest, and I left him to die. Jones wouldn't have done it. He's spineless."

William shook his head and laughed. "Spineless? Are you certain? Yes, I see how all this will play out." He glanced at the doctor, ignoring the next wave that swirled around their boots up to the ankles. "The Crown's agents are closing in. You need to get out from under Hawley's thumb. No one else knows of your treachery. Once Hawley shoots me, you'll shoot him. And what story will you concoct to the authorities? Or tell Aislin?"

"Shut up, m'lord! You don't know what you're talking about." But the doctor's hand trembled, causing his pistol to shake.

Gad, what a situation. They were all holding pistols on each other.

Two trained on him.

His was firmly trained on Hawley, for this heir to a duke was a ruthless killer. There would be no talking his way out of death with this man. But the doctor's hand was still unsteady. He was an odd mix of healer and tortured soul. Hopefully, not the sort to kill a man in cold blood.

"Dr. Jones and I have been working together for about a year now," Hawley boasted, but his gaze darted to the doctor often enough that William knew he'd firmly planted that seed of doubt.

He could tell by the cold glint in Hawley's eyes that he had similar intentions. Two villains ready to turn on each other. If Hawley had his way, this Welshman would also be dead tonight.

William meant to take full advantage. "How long do you think this will go on, Dr. Jones? Lord Hawley has no intention of continuing to pay you to remain silent. Your blackmail days are coming to an end. You've outlived your usefulness and are becoming a liability."

"Shut up, Whitpool." The doctor's voice had a shrill rasp to it.

William eased back, knowing he ought not push too hard, or he'd be shot before he got his answers. He addressed Hawley. "Tell me what happened that night. How did you lure Gideon here?"

"Does it matter?" Hawley asked, his lips still twisted in a sneer.

"Yes. He was my little brother." William's heart was breaking.

He might have saved Gideon, if only he'd come sooner.

Why hadn't Gideon sent word to him?

Why hadn't he sent word to anyone in the family?

Hawley spoke up first, ignoring the waves now steadily licking at their boots. "We lured him down here by pretending we'd abducted Aislin. We knew she was working with him to take down the Cornish pirates. Of course, he thought he was coming to her rescue."

William listened numbly to the rest.

"I shot him at the very spot you're standing now. Dr. Jones remained behind to make certain his body washed out to sea. I could not stay to see it all play out. Dawn was breaking, and I had to return to the Pendragon Inn, slipping back in the same way I'd gone out, unseen through the secret passageway the Sloanes use to smuggle goods in and out of their establishment." Hawley nodded toward the doctor. "I dared not be seen with *him* by the caves. Too many questions raised. But I strolled down here the following day, collecting some rather pretty shells while I made certain no trace of your brother remained."

"And Aislin knew nothing of this?"

The doctor laughed. "Oh, I'm sure she suspected something. Why else would she come here every day for all these weeks? But she never suspected me."

"Or me," Hawley intoned. "I doubt she's ever noticed me. Your brother would never allow me to come with him to their secret meetings. But a word of caution, Whitpool. I wouldn't get too close to the lass. Unless you and your brother like to share your conquests."

"A meaningless warning since I'll be dead within a few minutes." He ignored the bastard's laughter and the insult to Aislin. It was only meant to rile him. "Dr. Jones, what did you give Aislin? Was it poison?"

"Yes. I'm afraid she'll be dead by the time I return."

Blessed saints.

"I didn't wish to harm her. I like the girl, but I had no choice. She knows too much."

Thank goodness she'd had the foresight to toss away the draught. "How will you explain her body in your infirmary? Her father will skin you alive."

"Oh, she won't be found there. Someone will find her floating in the sea tomorrow morning. The poor, mad girl will have taken her own life."

William quietly palmed the knife tucked up his sleeve. "I don't know, Doctor. Sounds to me as if you're both getting desperate. Two bodies found on the same night? Me shot. Aislin drowned. Too much of a coincidence. Gentleman Jack will not believe it."

"We'll take that risk," Hawley said, steadying his aim. But he did not fire his pistol. "Jones, kill him."

William turned to the doctor. "Don't! He'll kill you as soon as you've taken care of me. Make him take the shot."

Hawley's features twisted in rage. "Shut up, you arrogant bastard!"

Three men. Three pistols. Two aimed at him. But his weapon remained trained on Hawley. Fear of being shot himself was all that kept the man from shooting William in that moment.

And Jones feared to spend his shot, knowing Hawley would then kill him.

This was rich! A standoff.

"Have I hit on a sore spot, Hawley? Ruined your plans? They're ruined anyway. No one will believe Dr. Jones is the high-level agent turned traitor, even if they do find Aislin dead in his infirmary. He's just a lackey. No Welshman would ever be admitted into the highest circles."

William pressed on. "But *Mr. Worthington* has gone to Trevena regularly to visit the doctor. And the doctor has gone to the Pendragon Inn to treat Mr. Worthington for some feigned illness or other. You're the outsider, Hawley. Suspicion will immediately fall on you. And Maisie will tearfully confess she was the one who told you about the smuggler's passageway. Will you kill everyone in Boscastle to keep them quiet?"

"Stop talking or I'll shoot!"

"No, you won't. Because the doctor will shoot you as soon as you've taken me down. You're done here. All you can do now is run, for Gentleman Jack will put it all together and come after both of you. And when he catches you, as he certainly will, he'll rip you apart with his bare hands. Slowly. In a manner that will cause you unimaginably excruciating pain. You should not have hurt his daughter."

Hawley startled as a wave suddenly washed over him, soaking his elegant pants up to the knees.

William smiled. "Gentlemen, the tide's coming in fast. How long before we are all drowned? Shall we take this fight to the beach?"

"No." Another wave swirled around Hawley, soaking him to the hips. He moved deeper into the cave, stepping onto higher ground close to where the doctor stood. In the next moment, he shot the doctor and grabbed his pistol before kicking his lifeless body to the ground.

William was about to launch his dagger through Hawley's heart when a shot rang out.

William stared at the dagger still in his palm. He clutched his own heart, certain Hawley must have shot him. But he felt no pain. No burn on any part of his body. Was he too numb to notice? He patted his chest again. Nothing.

Sweet Mother!

Hawley hadn't taken a shot. He lay dead on the rocks beside the lifeless doctor.

William was untouched.

Aislin.

He called out her name.

"William, are you hurt?" She limped to his side.

He swept her up in his arms, just as a wave was about to knock her down. "No, love. Thanks to you. I ought to throttle you for disobeying me, but I'm too grateful at the moment."

She put her arms around him, careful to keep the pistol she was still clutching pointed away from him. "It wasn't me. I didn't fire that shot, although I was about to. My pistol is still loaded. I thought you had done it."

"No, my weapon is…hell." He nudged her behind him.

Who had shot Hawley?

Chapter Nine

"GIDEON, DAMN IT. Come out where I can see you." William hoped it was his brother and not Gentleman Jack come in search of his missing daughter.

To his relief, the big oaf who stepped out of the shadows was indeed his brother. Much unchanged, although he appeared a little broader in the shoulders, truly full grown into a man.

William went to him and wrapped him in a fierce embrace. "You have a lot of explaining to do."

His brother hugged him back with equal ferocity. "I know. Let's head back to the Pendragon Inn and we'll talk."

"No," Aislin said, struggling to maintain her balance as wave after wave began to roll in. "I have to return to my father."

The cave was quickly filling with water. Within a few minutes, there would be no escape. William grabbed Aislin and lifted her into his arms as another wave was about to knock her down. "I'm not letting you out of my sight ever again."

Gideon reloaded his pistol before tucking it safely away. "The militia will have surrounded the Farnsworth Inn by now. They're presently rounding up every pirate found within the walls of Port Isaac. The crooked officials as well."

"My father," Aislin said in a ragged whisper and clung tightly to William as they battled against the surging tide to make their way onto the safety of the beach.

Gideon urged them to keep walking. "We mustn't stay out in the open."

They made their way to the steps leading up to the castle. "I'm sorry, Aislin," Gideon said as they climbed, their boots and clothing drenched, but none of them were complaining, for they were happy to be alive. "There is nothing I can do for him. He'll be taken into custody along with the other pirates."

"You planned this raid for tonight? How is it possible Hawley was not aware?" she asked.

William was thinking the same thing, for Hawley seemed only to be worried about the doctor and how to be rid of him.

Gideon did not break his stride as they climbed. "Hawley believed he'd killed me. He left Dr. Jones behind to make certain the deed was done, but the coward ran off soon after Hawley did. I almost feel sorry for the Welshman, he's a blackmailer but not a killer. Lucky for me."

William frowned. "He gave Aislin poison to drink."

Gideon's eyes rounded, and he cast Aislin a look of surprise. "Damn, his desperation must have pushed him over the brink."

Aislin nodded. "I wasn't going to drink anything he gave me. Go on, Gideon. Tell us the rest of it."

"Anyway, I survived, swam out of the cave before it filled with water, and then immediately reported to our Home Office. Hawley was so full of himself; he didn't consider for a moment his shot had missed my heart."

William frowned. "But he must have seen blood on you."

"He got me in the shoulder. Hurt like blazes, it did. The blood spurted onto my chest. Once the Home Office knew he was the elusive traitor and that Dr. Jones was his accomplice, we prepared to mount our operation."

William paused on the steps. "Cutting both of them out of the planning?"

"We fed them useless information, hoping they would not suspect we were on to them. I had to stay in hiding. None of this would have worked unless they both believed me dead."

Aislin frowned. "Why didn't you let me know?"

"Because Dr. Jones had to believe you were worried and frantic. We had this operation planned to the last detail...except we hadn't considered William showing up when he did." He shook his head and laughed softly. "We had to scramble to move up the raids. What made you come here now, Will?"

William smiled at Aislin, shifting her more securely in his arms. "A dream."

Gideon frowned. "A what?"

"He'll explain later," Aislin said with a gentle laugh. "Well, it's done now. We're safe. But my father...I hadn't thought I'd care. But I do. What will become of him?"

William understood her conflicted feelings, of hating the man for the pirate he was and at the same time, loving him for the father he'd been to her. Even though Gentleman Jack always thought of himself first, there was no question, he'd raised Aislin as a beloved daughter.

He supposed even the cruelest pirate could find a place in his heart for his children.

Gideon held up his torch as they reached the castle ruins.

William refused to let Aislin out of his arms. Nor did he wish to lose Gideon so soon after finding him. "Our horses are tethered by the infirmary. At least, they were. I don't know if they are still."

Gideon nodded. "Wait here. I'll fetch them."

As his brother took off, William set Aislin down on one of the castle stones and finally allowed himself to feel a moment of relief. He settled beside her and wrapped his arms around her to try to warm her up. She was wet and shivering even though the night was warm and there was little breeze to speak of.

He was worried, fearing she'd exerted herself too much and

torn the stitches Dr. Jones had taken care to sew. He'd actually done a good job of tending to her wound. What a waste to lose a good healer, but this Welshman deserved to die. He'd given Aislin the poison concoction to drink.

William would have cut out his heart while it was still beating, if he'd survived.

Blessed Mother, he was grateful Aislin had the presence of mind not to drink it.

Was she bleeding again?

"I'm going to marry you, Aislin. I'm going to raise a family with you and live out a long, dull, and happy life with you by my side. The duller, the better."

She lifted her head off his shoulder and laughed. "That does not sound at all appealing."

"You know what I mean. I'm speaking of our day-to-day life." The nights spent in passionate exploration of her body would be anything but dull. "I don't wish for excitement other than in our marriage bed."

"Ye'll have to gain my permission first," a man's harsh voice resounded among the ruins.

"Jack!" Aislin leaped to her feet. "Ouch." Her leg buckled, and she would have fallen if William hadn't caught her.

"Are ye hurt, daughter?"

"No, Jack."

William drew her behind him, his pistol drawn, and heart pounding a hole through his chest. How had this man escaped the noose closing in on Port Isaac? She'd called him Jack, no doubt refusing to acknowledge him as her father after he'd destroyed William's ship and all the innocent sailors on it.

"Put down yer weapon, m'lord. I'm unarmed. Forgive and forget, is what I say. Where's yer damn brother? I'm here to talk to him."

"He's gone for our horses," Aislin replied. "Promise me you're unarmed and won't hurt Baron Whitpool. Promise on my mother's grave."

To William's surprise, he nodded. "Aye, Aislin. I swear it on yer sainted mother's grave."

William did not lower his pistol, preferring to keep it trained on Gentleman Jack even after Gideon returned and they all rode back to the Pendragon Inn. It was nearing dawn. The sky had lightened, and the sun was peering over the cloudless horizon as they trotted into the inn's courtyard.

The scent of oats and biscuits and roasting pork emanated from the kitchen.

"Maisie, fetch us ales all around," Aislin's father said, giving the girl a wink when she opened the door to greet them.

She cast him a seductive smile. "Yes, Captain Farnsworth."

Aislin's father strode in as though he owned the place. He took a seat in the common room as though presiding over a business meeting. His familiarity with Maisie was obvious and not in any fatherly way. When she delivered the ale, he tossed her a coin. "Gentlemen, won't you join me?" He began to casually sip from the tankard just set before him.

The girl licked her lips and smiled suggestively at Gideon who had yet to sit. He preferred to stand guard over Aislin's father whom none of them trusted. "You're a good lass, Maisie," Gideon muttered, also tossing her a coin.

Giggling, she darted back into the kitchen.

William spared a glance at his brother, who merely grinned and shrugged.

Sighing, William returned his attention to Aislin's father. Gentleman Jack Farnsworth was a big man, scarred about the mouth and eyes. He had thick dark hair and sported a beard as black as a raven's wing.

As black as Aislin's hair, but hers was long and silky while his was thick and matted.

Nor were his eyes her soft gray.

His were dark as coal. Devil's eyes.

He was dressed elegantly, as though having purposely donned his finery for a special occasion. The special occasion would be his hanging, if it were up to William. But Gideon was in charge here, so he merely sat back and watched.

He had to give Gentleman Jack credit. The man showed no sign of fear. He spoke with a casual wave of his hand. The rings on his fingers and those in his ear gleamed by the early, morning firelight.

William glanced around to make certain this pirate had brought none of his crew along. He noticed Gideon doing the same.

"I came on my own," Gentleman Jack said, his voice deep and raspy. "As I've told ye already, I'm unarmed."

Aislin moved to sit beside her father, but William held her back. "Sit here." In truth, he wanted her upstairs and out of the way, but he knew better than to demand it. She was not ready to leave her father's side just yet.

William sat between them. It was the best he could do to protect this girl who did not wish to be protected. In truth, he doubted Jack would harm his own daughter. No, he and Gideon were his intended victims, assuming he meant to kill them now. He did not believe for a moment the man had no weapon on him, even though Gideon had searched him earlier.

William still had his pistol trained on the man, discretely under the table. He'd shoot him in the gut if he so much as twitched an eye.

Aislin frowned at her father. "I have a few words to say to you." She rolled up her sleeves. "How did you escape the militia?"

"As fate would have it, I'd heard ye'd been injured, and I was on my way to Trevena to rescue ye. I was in the hills outside of Port Isaac when I heard shots and saw a vessel on fire in the harbor. I knew the militia was finally coming after us. But all I cared about was getting to ye, lass. Ye're my daughter. My treasure. Seems the baron got to ye before I did." He quirked a bushy eyebrow. "Did ye know about the raid, lass?"

"No, Jack. I only learned of it about an hour ago." She tipped her chin up. "I'm not sorry though. You all deserve to hang. You deserve far worse."

"Now, lass. Ye–"

"I mean it, Jack. You killed so many innocent souls." She stared down this dangerous man. William tightened his grasp on the pistol, only to ease it a moment later. There was something in her father's expression. He wasn't here to hurt them or his daughter.

He was here for exactly the reason he'd stated earlier at Tintagel Castle—to negotiate.

What information could he possibly have to earn himself a pardon? He'd probably make something up, anything to implicate someone important and save his own hide.

Aislin's father cast him an icy stare. "I didn't want to kill any of them, only you, Whitpool. Yet, you still live."

William returned his icy stare. "Despite your efforts."

Tears formed in Aislin's eyes. "How could you do this to him? Destroy his life because I looked upon him with affection? He had already sailed with the tide. He was never coming back to me."

"Aislin, my child. Do ye not understand? Ye set his blood afire. He was always coming back for ye. He's here now, isn't he? I never doubted he'd come for ye. I had to stop him."

"Because of the way I looked at him?"

"It was never about that." Her father emitted a ragged breath. "It was about the way *he* looked at ye, lass. The same way I looked at yer mother when I first set eyes on her. Ye resemble her. Same long, dark hair. Same silver-gray eyes. The day I first saw her, I thought I was looking upon a dream. That's how Whitpool looked at ye. As though ye were his dream. I couldn't let him steal ye from me."

Aislin began to cry softly. "He never would have."

"Do ye think I'm blind, daughter? He wanted ye, and he was determined to have ye. Just as I did yer mother. But my intentions were honorable. I married her."

"What made you think Baron Whitpool would not marry me?"

"Ye just said it, he's a baron. The likes of us will never be good enough for the likes of him. He meant to take ye, but never as his wife. How else was I to protect ye?"

"There were other ways" She used her sleeve to wipe the tears off her cheeks. "Certainly not by killing him."

"I had to do something, didn't I? I'll never let any man use ye and then cast ye off."

"You're wrong, Jack." She still refused to acknowledge him as her father. "He would have married me. He's already asked me. But I can never accept him now, not after what you did to him and his crew. I don't know why he shows me any kindness, knowing who I am. I don't know why he should care what ill befalls me."

William took her hand. "Aislin, this changes nothing between us."

"Do you hear yourself? This changes *everything*. My father will go to prison. He'll likely be hanged before the month is out. Everything he owns will be confiscated." She buried her head in her hands and let out a wrenching sob. "Gideon, tell him. Talk sense into your brother."

"No, Aislin. He's chosen wisely for himself."

"Then you are both fools." She looked up at them through her tears and frowned. "When the fog lifts and he remembers what happened, he will grow to hate me."

Her father groaned. "No, Aislin. He won't. He'll remember ye tried to save him. He'll remember the way his heart soared the moment he set eyes on ye. Do ye not understand? I was wrong about him. Marry the man and protect yerself. He'll always love ye, my child. I've just told ye what ye mean to him. Ye are his heart.

His very soul."

His dream.

In the next moment, he slapped his hands on the table and turned to William's brother. "Ye're the one they call Gideon Croft. Now that we're about to be family, sit down and let's make a deal. Hawley isn't the only traitor. I'll give ye names in exchange for a full pardon."

Gideon pulled out the chair opposite his and sank into it. "Gentleman Jack, I expected no less from you. Tell me what you know."

Chapter Ten

ONE WEEK LATER, Aislin stood beneath one of the archways of Tintagel Castle holding sprigs of pink roses and heather in her hands. She wore a gown adorned with ivory lace and a circlet of meadow flowers in her hair.

The morning sun shone down upon the castle, casting it and the turquoise sea below in a golden light.

Even the castle stones, so dark and ancient, seemed to glow.

"Are you ready, Aislin?" William took her hand and turned to face the minister who stood before them with Bible in hand.

Gideon and Mr. Musgrove served as their witnesses. A handful of friends from Polzeath and Port Isaac were in attendance, those fortunate enough to have escaped the militia's raids. There were twenty or so in all.

Aislin had eyes only for William, this big, handsome man who wanted to walk through life with her.

The ceremony took place by special license, a necessity since they both wished their wedding to occur here, amid the majestic ruins where William's dreams had led him.

They stood under a perfect, Celtic blue sky. He cast her a tender smile. "I love you, my Aislin."

That's what he called her now. *My Aislin.*

She smiled up at him, noticing the lightness in his emerald

eyes. "I love you, too."

Gideon sniffled behind them.

William turned to his brother. "Don't cry, you arse. I'll never be able to stay angry with you if you do."

"Shut up and marry the girl. Don't make too much of it. The sun's in my eyes, that's all. You can beat me up later about my abandoning Abby. I had no idea Peter was in such bad shape. But we'll all be together again at Christmastide. A family reunited. Although Aislin's father will not join us. He'll spend the rest of his days under house arrest."

"Where he deserves to be," Aislin muttered.

"He's a resourceful man. I venture he'll have his lands and ships back and be a privateer for the Crown within a month's time," William said.

"He's turned over some important names," Gideon acknowledged with a grunt. "But the government clerks work slowly. I give it two months before he's freed. Now is not the time to speak of him. Kiss Aislin and stop looking at me. If you hug me one more time, I'm going to punch you."

"You're a monumental arse, Gideon."

"So are you, big brother." He sniffled again and quickly cleared his throat. "But I'm glad you're alive. I can't think of anyone I'd rather insult."

Aislin could not suppress her laughter.

She wanted boys just like these two brothers. Smart and stubborn. Ready to hurl teasing insults at each other and yet run through the fires of hell to save each other. She understood why Gideon had not returned to his family or claimed the title when he thought William had been killed. He was ashamed. He believed he'd failed to save William and blamed himself for his beloved brother's death.

So, he worked tirelessly to bring down the pirates who had claimed William's life.

Aislin shook her head to clear away these sad thoughts. Each brother had suffered torments believing the other was dead. But they were reunited now. She could see the love they held for each other revealed in the gleam of their eyes.

Gideon was a handsome man.

But William was perfection. He was the mate to her soul.

As evening fell and everyone returned to their homes, she and William returned to the Pendragon Inn. She was now undressing in William's chamber, assisted only by him. His hands were warm, the pads of his fingers calloused as he ran them through her hair and then slowly, ever so slowly, over her body.

His gaze was fiery as he unlaced her gown, scorching as he swept her hair aside and kissed her on the neck. "My dreams were always of you, my Aislin. I had no memory of my name. No memory of the burns on my leg and shoulders. No memory of my past. But I always remembered you."

His kisses were rich and intense, even the gentle ones he trailed along her neck. This big, handsome man whose body was forged of iron knew how to stir her blood, knew how to make her respond to his touch. It still amazed her that he loved her, that he'd known it the moment they met.

How could she possibly matter to him?

And yet, she did.

He released her suddenly and stood staring at her...through her.

"William, what's wrong?"

He raked his fingers through his hair. "How did I know to find you at Tintagel Castle? I'd only ever seen you in Port Isaac. But my dreams were of you among the castle ruins."

She smiled. "You don't remember what I told you after I warned you about my father?"

He cast her a blank stare. "No. What did you tell me?"

She wiped a tear that had spilled from the corner of her eye. "I said I would ride to Tintagel Castle to watch your ship sail off. I wanted to be sure you'd made it safely away. *I'll be at Tintagel Castle.* That's what I promised you. Those were my last words to you. This is what you remembered."

"It's what my heart remembered." He stripped out of his own clothes, all but his trousers. His body was magnificent. She wanted to touch him, run her hands along his muscled arms and kiss the scarred skin along his shoulders.

He was as eager to touch her, his hands on her hips, sliding up to her waist, skimming over her breasts as he slipped the gossamer chemise over her head.

He tossed it aside, his gaze never leaving her body. She blushed and tried to cover herself with her hair, for it was long, and she'd worn it unbound, as always.

"Aislin," he whispered, his voice raw. He buried his fingers in her hair and brought her forward for his kiss.

Sweet mercy! The touch of his mouth on hers was anything but tame. His kiss was molten, the heat of it like lava pouring into an untamed sea.

He carried her to their bed, taking a moment to remove the last of his clothes. When he turned away to unbutton his trousers, she studied the burn scars on his shoulders. She'd kissed them and run her hands lightly over them just moments before. These scars would always be a reminder of the evil her father had inflicted upon him.

He must have suffered greatly. They still looked very bad, but she wouldn't allow him to hide them from her. "Don't, Aislin," he said when she reached out to touch them again.

"They are a part of you. They made you the man you are to-day." His body was more perfect for these imperfections.

She saw the flash of pain in his eyes. "I'm a man with no memory of the most important part of his life."

"No, our future is what matters most. We'll make new memories together. Come, my love. Join me in bed."

He willingly obliged, settling over her so that she felt the splendid weight of him against her body.

He looked upon her as though he was a man famished.

"Lady Whitpool," he whispered, smiling, "I love you."

"I love you, too, Baron Whitpool." She wrapped her arms around his shoulders where the fiery wood from the ship breaking apart had struck him as it fell into the sea. "No need to be gentle. You will not hurt me."

But he insisted on it because of her leg.

Mother in heaven. What this man's touch did to her. He teased her with his mouth and deft fingers, so she was ready and crying out for him.

He growled in satisfaction when he entered her and began to move inside her with the magnificent grace of a lion. Her body responded with a craven wanting, her blood turning thick. "William!"

She burrowed against his body, taking in the heat and power of him, the beautiful strength of him as he sought his own release which came on the heels of hers. He held her in his arms. Swallowed her up in them, for they were as big as oak trees, providing strength and shelter.

He emitted a feral growl when he was spent and collapsed atop her.

The crush of his body on hers felt splendid. But he quickly rolled aside and lifted her so that she now lay atop him. She rested her cheek against his chest, not minding that the light spray of gold hairs across his chest tickled her skin.

She nestled against his body, lulled by the steady beat of his heart. "You are all muscle and heat."

He chuckled, obviously pleased with his performance...or hers...or both. He took her into his embrace and began to stroke her hair. "You are softness and silk," he said, closing his eyes a moment.

"What are you thinking, William?"

He opened them to stare at her, then tucked a finger under her chin and drew her lips to his for a searing kiss. "I lay floating in the water, my back burned and bruised, and all hope lost. I felt myself slipping into the sea. Then you called to me. You held on to me, somehow. I don't know how, but you were beside me until I was rescued."

"Is that when your dream of me began?"

"Yes." He kissed her again. "It's a good feeling."

"What is, my love?"

"Knowing that my dream came true."

Also by Meara Platt

About the Author

Meara Platt is an award winning, USA Today bestselling author and an Amazon UK All-star. Her favorite place in all the world is England's Lake District, which may not come as a surprise since many of her stories are set in that idyllic landscape, including her paranormal romance Dark Gardens series. If you'd like to learn more about the ancient Fae prophecy that is about to unfold in the Dark Gardens, as well as Meara's lighthearted, international bestselling Regency romances in the Book of Love, Farthingale, and Braydens series, please visit Meara's website at www.mearaplatt. com.

Made in the USA
Columbia, SC
08 May 2025

57702056R00063